Mordecai C. Cooke

A Plain and Easy Account of British Fungi

with descriptions of the esculent and poisonous species - and a tabular

arrangement of orders and genera

Mordecai C. Cooke

A Plain and Easy Account of British Fungi
with descriptions of the esculent and poisonous species - and a tabular arrangement of
orders and genera

ISBN/EAN: 9783337387242

Printed in Europe, USA, Canada, Australia, Japan

Cover: Foto ©Andreas Hilbeck / pixelio.de

More available books at **www.hansebooks.com**

A PLAIN AND EASY ACCOUNT

OF

BRITISH FUNGI:

WITH

DESCRIPTIONS OF THE ESCULENT AND POISONOUS SPECIES,
DETAILS OF THE PRINCIPLES OF SCIENTIFIC
CLASSIFICATION,

AND

A TABULAR ARRANGEMENT OF ORDERS AND GENERA.

BY

M. C. COOKE,

AUTHOR OF "A MANUAL OF STRUCTURAL BOTANY,"
"A MANUAL OF BOTANIC TERMS," ETC.

WITH TWENTY-FOUR COLOURED PLATES.

LONDON:
ROBERT HARDWICKE, 192, PICCADILLY.

1862.

PREFACE.

It is sometimes necessary for a writer to give some reasons for inflicting a new work upon the public, while treatises on the same subject are already in print ; but from this necessity I am in the present instance absolved by the fact that no popular work on this branch of Botany exists, or, to my knowledge, has hitherto been attempted. With all its failings, therefore, this effort has the merit of *novelty* to commend it, and I trust it will hereafter be found of *utility* also. The difficulties to be encountered in describing, with as little technicality as possible, the different species of esculent fungi—so that persons unacquainted therewith may discriminate them —have been much diminished by the liberality with which the publisher has illustrated this work. Whilst endeavouring to render the subject acceptable to the general reader, I have at the same time kept the botanical student in view ; and if, in the laudable attempt to make this a "Plain and Easy Account of British Fungi" for both classes of readers, I should have failed in making it of service to either, it will at least serve to familiarize the one with the fact that hundredweights of good food are annually wasted, and the other it will furnish with a synopsis of classification based upon the researches of some of the most eminent mycologists of the age.

That there is ample room for such a work as the present will not be denied ; but whether that desideratum is now efficiently supplied, is not for me to determine.

Let me assure the student that all times, seasons, and localities, will afford him some species for examination ; and whether he has felt interested in them before, or now, for the first time, adopts these interesting plants as objects worthy of his special regard, I would commend them to his patient and persevering attention, in the assurance that this pursuit will "lead from joy to joy."

M. C. C.

Twickenham Economic Museum.

CONTENTS.

PLATES.

BRITISH FUNGI.

To some—and we would hope that the number is few—the very name of Fungus is unknown. To others this name is associated only with the pileated species, or at most with the addition of puff-balls, or such as possess a truly fungoid odour. There doubtless may be found a privileged few, amongst the unscientific denizens of our islands, who acknowledge a broader view, and include a far less limited series of these extraordinary productions of the vegetable kingdom within the terms of our title.

It would be vain to attempt a general and compact definition of a fungus, or to describe in a few words what is included in the large group to which the name of Fungi is given, so as to be popularly intelligible. The contents of the present volume must be left to perform this office for us, or so much of it as remains untold after we have pointed out some of the most characteristic of the homes of the race.

It is indeed a singular and despised family to the history of which we are about to dedicate this volume. Many of those who would merit the title of "good

B

botanists" know little or nothing about them. That part of our scientific literature which is devoted to them is remarkably scanty; and the young student, or the operative botanist, whose means are limited, inquires in vain for assistance in gaining even a slight knowledge of a very interesting section of our Flora. For such we can scarce hope to accomplish much; but even this little may not prove unwelcome. Whilst manuals of flowering plants, with or without illustrations, are abundant, no corresponding guides to cryptogams can be found equally complete, cheap, or useful.

The Spitalfields weaver, who gets away into the country whenever a half-holiday falls to his lot, for the purpose of adding to his humble herbarium, or becoming better acquainted with the Flora of his native land, must look upon the lichen or fungus as objects reserved for the study of those who can better afford the necessary literary assistance. Although this may still be asserted, with equal justice, when our work is accomplished; yet if we succeed in exciting an interest amongst only a few readers, this may hasten the time when the desideratum shall be supplied.

To say that fungi may be found everywhere, would not perhaps be always literally true; but to say where they are *not* to be found, under any circumstances, would be puzzling. Not only are shady woods, mossy dells, secluded lanes, and green pastures, the habitats of fungi, but we meet with them in almost every situation where vegetable life is possible, and traces

of them where it is not. Wherever decaying vegetable matter exists, we may expect to find a new
race flourishing amid the *débris*, as in the decay
of the garden of " the sensitive plant " described
by Shelley :—

> And plants at whose name the verse feels loath,
> Fill'd the place with a monstrous undergrowth,
> Prickly and pulpous, and blistering, and blue,
> Livid, and starr'd with a lurid dew,
>
> And agarics, and fungi, with mildew and mould,
> Started like mist from the wet ground cold;
> Pale, fleshy, as if the decaying dead
> With a spirit of growth had been animated.
>
> Their mass rotted off them flake by flake,
> Till the thick stalk stuck like a murderer's stake,
> Where rags of loose flesh yet tremble on high,
> Infecting the winds that wander by.

Such a spot is an almost certain home for fungi.
Every rotten stump or twig, every decaying leaf or fruit,
has its peculiar species,—some large enough to attract
immediate attention, others so small as to be invisible
to the unaided eye. But we need not travel from home
to meet with examples: the unwelcome dry-rot may
have committed its ravages beneath our kitchen floor;
or the walls of our cellars, and our casks, or bottles of
wine, may be infested with members of this ubiquitous
race. Can we find no morsel of bread or cheese upon
which a mould is flourishing? no towel or other article
of household linen presenting traces of mildew? Are
we perfectly certain that all our preserves are unvisited?

or, to come nearer to some of us, all our books un-
touched ?

But, in places which many would consider more un-
likely still, we may look for and expect to find fungi:*
on whitewashed walls, plaster ceilings, dirty glass, old
flannel, and old boots and shoes, or leather of any
description ; on carpets, mats, and boards, and even the
plants in our herbaria must be watched against their
ravages.   Animals bear them about on their horns and
hoofs, and the housefly often carries in its body the
vegetating fungus which ultimately deprives it of life.
The yeast that is employed for fermenting our bread
and our beer is a fungus, as well as the mildew and
smut that infest our growing corn.

From cesspools and traps the minute dust-like spores
of hidden fungi rise into our dwellings, unseen they
float in the air, entering everywhere, depositing themselves everywhere, and vegetating wherever the conditions are favourable to their development.

It was strongly affirmed at one time that our cholera
visitations were due to these invisible agents, and a
large volume has been written on these vegetable
parasites on men and animals.   " When our beer
becomes mothery, the mother of that mischief is a

* As a difficulty is occasionally experienced amongst amateurs
with reference to the pronunciation of this word in its plural
form, we may remind them, that in the singular the *g* should be
hard, as in *gum*, whilst in the plural *fungi* has the *g* soft, as
Fun-ji. It may be permitted us to protest against such a bar-
barism as *funguses*, which has sometimes been employed as the
plural of *fungus*.

fungus; if pickles acquire a bad taste, if ketchup turns ropy and putrefies, fungi have a finger in it all. Their reign stops not here—they even prey on each other. The close cavities of nuts occasionally afford concealment to some species ; others, like leeches, stick to the bulbs of plants, and suck them dry ; and some pick timber to pieces as men pick oakum." Hop-mildew, vine-disease, turnip-mildew, bunt, smut, ergot, potato-murrain, pea and wheat mildew, may all be traced to them as the fertile source of mischief.

That fungi may be developed under, apparently, the most unfavourable circumstances, may be gathered from an instance recorded by Schweinitz, of a blacksmith at Salem, who, having thrown on one side a piece of iron which he had just taken from the fire, was called off to some other business, and on his return in the morning was astonished to see on this very piece, lying over the water on his smith's trough, a mass of fungi two feet in length. It had crept from the iron to some adjacent wood, and not from the wood to the iron. This immense mass had grown during the space of twelve hours. The Rev. M. J. Berkeley also found a species of fungus vegetating on a lead cistern at Kew; and Sowerby, the author of an illustrated work on British Fungi, published more than half a century since, found a species growing on some cinders on the outside of the dome of St. Paul's.

Nor are these plants less worthy of notice on account of the rapidity of their growth. The great Puff Ball springs up in a marvellous manner to the size of a pumpkin during the night; and Dr. Lindley has computed that the cells of which its structure is composed have multiplied at the extraordinary rate of sixty millions in a minute. Dr. Greville mentions an instance of one of the largest of our British fungi (*Polyporus squamosus*) attaining a circumference of seven feet five inches, and weighing thirty-four pounds, after having been cut four days. It was only four weeks in attaining to these dimensions, thus acquiring an increase of growth equal to nineteen ounces per day. During the past summer we noticed an individual of this same species which reached a diameter of eleven inches within the short space of a week. Blue-mould is also rapid in its growth, although the plant individually is small, and a meadow or pasture which in the evening exhibited no prominent signs of mushrooms, may in the morning yield a good basket-full. The popular notion, current in some agricultural districts, that fungi melt away when the sun shines upon them, sends the mushroom-gatherer to seek them

> " When the grass is wet with dew,
> In the morning early."

Dr. Carpenter relates an instance of the expansive power resulting from the rapid growth of the soft cellular tissue of fungi which seems marvellous. Some years ago the town of Basingstoke was paved; and not many months afterwards the pavement was observed to exhibit an unevenness which could not easily be accounted for. In a short time after, the mystery was explained, for some of the heaviest stones were completely lifted out of their beds by the growth of large toadstools beneath them. One of these stones measured twenty-two inches by twenty-one, and weighed eighty-three pounds, and the resistance afforded by the mortar which held it in its place would probably be even a greater obstacle than the weight. It became necessary to repave the whole town in consequence of this remarkable disturbance. A similar incident came under our own notice, of a large kitchen hearthstone which was forced up from its bed by an under-growing fungus, and had to be relaid two or three times, until at last it reposed in peace, the old bed having been removed to the depth of six inches, and a new foundation laid. A circumstance recorded by Sir Joseph Banks is still more extraordinary, of a cask of wine which, having been confined for three years in a cellar, was, at the termination of that period, found to have leaked from the cask and vegetated in the form of immense fungi, which had filled the cellar and borne upwards the empty wine-cask to the roof.

It is a curious fact in connection with the growth of these singular plants, that, while Phanærogams absorb carbonic acid from the atmosphere, and respire oxygen, in this instance the order is reversed, and carbonic acid gas is given off. It is believed that the absence of green colouring matter, with the exception in some few instances of a kind of mineral green, is due, in part, to this reversal of transpired gases. One thing is certain, that in flowering plants light is absolutely essential not only to the growth and healthy condition of the plant, but also to the production of the green chlorophyl, or colouring matter. Fungi, on the contrary, would appear to flourish best in the absence of light, in dark cellars, under flagstones, in hollow trees, and in like places, where no other form of plant could exist ; while some genera are entirely subterranean.

The luminosity of fungi is a phenomenon which we do not often see exhibited in these temperate regions ; but in countries nearer the tropics it is not at all an uncommon occurrence for fungi to give out a kind of phosphorescent light with sufficient intensity to enable the traveller to read his letters or write up his journal.

> "And unctuous meteors from spray to spray
> Crept and flitted in broad noonday
> Unseen, every branch on which they alit
> By a venomous blight was burned and bit."

In our schoolboy days we remember to have often carried home in our pockets a piece of *touchwood*, to be taken to bed with us on account of the little light it afforded. What we, in common with our elders and betters, termed touchwood, was merely the light, white, decaying wood of an old stump, entirely permeated with the minute mycelium of a fungus, and which exhibited phosphorescence in the dark. The fact was well enough known to us, but the cause was a mystery ; the remotest idea of its being due to the presence of a fungoid growth never entered our boyish heads.

A kind of *Polyporus* (*P. sulfureus*), often found forming a dense mass on the stumps of trees, exhibits phosphorescence in the early stages of its decay.

The *forms* which these singular plants assume are extremely diversified: in some instances we have a distinct stem supporting a cap, and looking somewhat like a parasol; in others the stem is entirely absent, and the cap is attached either by its margin, and is said to be *dimidiate*, or by its back, or that which is more commonly its upper surface, when it is called *resupinate*. Sometimes the form and colour so nearly resemble that of a tongue, that, as Dr. Badham says, " in the days of enchanted trees you would not have cut it off to pickle or eat on any account, lest the knight to whom it belonged should afterwards come to claim it of you." In some species the form is that of a cup; in others of a goblet, a saucer, an ear, a birds-nest, a horn, a bunch of coral, a ball, a button, a rosette, a lump of jelly, or a piece of velvet. Indeed, so protean are they in shape, that description fails in giving an adequate idea of their variety.

In *colour* they are almost as variable as in shape: in one or two instances decidedly green; but this colour must be considered as rare amongst them. We have all shades of red, from light pink to deepest crimson; all tints of yellow, from sulphureous to orange; all kinds of browns, from palest ochre to deepest umber; and every gradation between pale grey and sooty black. Blue and violet tints do not abound; but even these, as well as a beautiful amethyst, occasionally occur. White or creamy tints are very common. There is a livid and suspicious shade to many of the species, not peculiarly attractive to the disinterested observer.

Odours are manifestly agreeable, or disagreeable, to a considerable extent, according to the taste of the inhaler; but it must be confessed that some of the fungi exhale an odour so intolerably fœtid, that no set of olfactory nerves could be found to endure it longer than was absolutely necessary. A lady having found a specimen of the truly elegant, but rare, *Clathrus*, set about making a sketch of it; but, notwithstanding her urgent desire to accomplish the task, she was compelled to have the fungus removed from the house before her sketch was finished.

A gentleman of our acquaintance, during a stroll through Darenth Wood, met with a specimen of the common stinkhorn (*Phallus impudicus*), which, having deposited in his sandwich-box and consigned to his pocket, he designed to take home and examine. For some time he had become conscious of an unpleasant odour; but it was not until he had entered the railway-carriage, to return to town, that he discovered the true source. Everybody in the compartment complained, and wondered what could be the cause, and quitted it as soon as an opportunity offered. Nothing but a resolute determination to make a drawing and section of the fungus could have prevented our friend throwing away stinkhorn and sandwich-box long ere his arrival in town; but, in this instance, botanical enthusiasm overcame all physical difficulties.

The fœtid or unpleasant odour is not, however, universal in fungi. There are some which have the scent of tarragon, of new-mown hay, of violets, of anise, of

walnuts, of new meal, &c. ; while there are others
which, we must confess, have the odour of onions, of
garlic, of tainted meat, of fish, and equally unpleasant
substances ; and others, again, which are devoid of any
perceptible odour. Some persons are very fond of
tasting, and here they may gratify that propensity ; for
in fungi they will meet with a variety of flavours, some
of which will be calculated to please and others to
disgust. In the raw state, probably, the acrid or
unpleasant prevails in the majority of cases, for some
species which are pleasant when cooked have a very
acrid taste when eaten raw. The number of poisonous
species has, perhaps, been exaggerated ; but of these
there are many, and the dangerous properties of
a few are extremely virulent. We have always
imagined it prudent to taste unknown species with
caution, since we have learnt that some mycologists
having, perhaps, more enthusiasm than caution, have,
from merely tasting very virulent species, suffered
for some time afterwards considerable pain and inconvenience. More especial reference will be made
hereafter to the species recommended as esculent, and
which may be found, in greater or less number, in our
own islands.

As articles of food, *fungi* are certainly deserving of
more attention than they have hitherto received from
the majority of our countrymen. People widely separated by mountains, oceans, or vast tracts of desert,
have been found employing certain species as delicacies.
Not only in China, as evidenced by the examples of

dried edible fungi sent to the International Exhibition of 1862, but also in the Himalayas and in the Rocky Mountains, as well as in Terra del Fuego, New Zealand, and Australia, to say nothing of European countries, certain species afford wholesome and nutritious food. Of their chemical composition we are very deficient in information. Few authentically-determined species have yet come under the cognizance of the chemist, and there is but little doubt that not only does the composition vary greatly in different species, as evidenced by their wholesome or unwholesome properties, but also in the same species under different conditions of climate and habitat, as well as during the different stages of its existence ; a few hours being sufficient in some cases to convert a wholesome food into a very injurious and, perhaps, dangerous substance.

GILL-BEARING FUNGI.

WITH a view to a more complete knowledge of the structure and arrangement of Fungi, it will be advisable to commence with an examination of one of the best known, as a type of the higher divisions of this interesting group of plants. Every one knows what a mushroom is, at least so far as regards its external appearance. If we carefully remove the soil from the base of the stem which bears the cap-like receptacle of mushrooms, we shall lay bare a number of pale entangled threads, which constitute the *mycelium* or spawn. These thread-like processes consist of a number of separate individuals which unitedly produce the stem already alluded to.

The mycelium of fungi is not always composed of filaments, but this kind will, for the present, serve the purpose of illustration. At certain points in this entangled mass of threads, a little rounded protuberance at first appears, which, as it enlarges, ruptures, and the young mushroom may be seen within it, with its cap or pileus supported upon its stem. The membrane which has up to this point inclosed the young mushroom is termed the *volva*, or wrapper, portions or traces of which often remain permanently at the base of the stem.

The young pileus or cap, for some time after it has emerged from the wrapper, retains its spherical or hemispherical form. As it expands, the under surface, which is seen to consist of a membrane, or in some cases only of a mass of entangled threads, ruptures, leaving a portion attached to the stem, or stipe, in the form of an irregular collar, ring, or annulus. This collar is in some species of Agaric permanent, in others it is moveable, whilst in a few it is entirely absent. The breaking away of the membrane from the under surface of the pileus, as already described, exposes a series of plates or gill-like processes, called also *lamellæ*, which radiate from the stem. These gills are covered with the fructifying surface, termed the *hymenium*, which bears the spores, or reproductive bodies.

The accompanying woodcut will make clearer the

position and relation of the parts we have described. At the base of this section of an Agaric the mycelium is

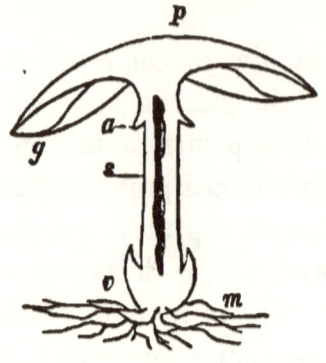

represented at *m*, proceeding from this the stipe or stem (*s*), surrounded by the remains of the *volva* or wrapper (*v*). The stem is surmounted by a *pileus* or cap (*p*), bearing *lamellæ* or gills on the under surface (*g*), which have been exposed by the disappearance of the indusium or veil, leaving traces in the form of an *annulus*, or ring, around the stem.

If we collect a specimen of mushroom, or any Agaric, and having separated the stem from the pileus, invert the latter, with the gills downwards, upon a piece of glass or a sheet of writing-paper, in the course of an hour or two a number of fine dust-like bodies will be seen to have fallen from the under surface of the pileus upon the glass or paper. These are the reproductive bodies, known as spores, which are borne upon the surface of the lamellæ. Their colour will in many instances be white, but in some of a purple tint, or various shades of brown. The further and more minute examination of these bodies requires the aid of a microscope.

It has been said that the spores of Agarics are borne upon what are termed the gills, and that the spore-bearing surface is called the hymenium. In the genus now under description this hymenium is folded or plaited

together in the form of a series of plates radiating from
the stem ; the two sides of these folds adhere more or
less by their backs, and in some species may be easily
opened out. Upon the surface of the hymenium will
be found a number of swollen threads or cells, called
sporophores, or basidia (*b*), each surmounted by four
smaller branches, termed spicules, or stigmata (*a*), each
of which is terminated by a spore. An immense number
of these spores are borne on the hymenium
of a single fungus, as will be evident by
the deposit obtained in the manner already
indicated. The spores vary not only in size,
but also in colour and form. Fries says
of them :—" They are so infinite—for in a single individual I have reckoned above 10,000,000—so subtile,
scarcely visible to the eye, and resembling thin smoke ;
so light, and are dispersed in so many ways, that it
is difficult to conceive a place from which they can be
excluded."

The whole of the description now concluded will
only apply to the *Agaricini*, or Gill-bearing Fungi. Of
these there are believed to exist at least one thousand
species, and one-tenth of them are probably esculent,
while perhaps one-sixth of them are not positively
unwholesome.

To determine the species to which any individual
Agaric may belong, it is necessary that the following
particulars should be noted—*i.e.*, whether found growing singly or in groups, and whether, if gregarious, it
formed a portion of a ring ; also, if found on the ground

or upon decaying wood, and whether rooting or not. It should carefully be noted if the stem is stout or slender, bulbous or fusiform, scaly, downy, or smooth ;

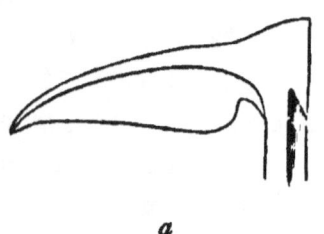

whether central in its insertion, eccentric, lateral, or almost obsolete ; what is the colour of the pileus, gills, and stem, the form of the pileus in the young as well as the mature plant ; and what is the nature of the surface of the pileus, whether downy or smooth, dull or shining, viscid or dry.   Then, by cutting the pileus and stem down the centre, the

a

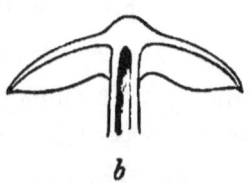

texture of both, their colour, and also whether the stem is fibrous, stuffed (*i.e.*, filled with a spongy or cottony mass) or fistulose (*i.e.*, hollow) (*a b*). The form and

b

position of the gills must also be noted. If their interior extremities are distant from the stem, they are *remote* (*c*) ; reaching the stem, but not attached thereto, *free*

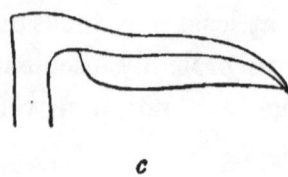

(*d*) ; but if attached, they are then termed *adnate* (*e*). If the gills run down the stem, they are said to be *decurrent* (*f*). Their opposite or outer extremity may be *forked*, or their interior toothed or

c

emarginate (*a*); and the whole surface of the gills may be narrow or broad, and they may be closely packed side by side, or *distant*.   And, finally, the colour of the spores and (if practicable) their form, as shown by the microscope should be determined.

This catalogue of desiderata will have intimated the points of variation which will be found in different species of *Agaricus*, and which will, some of them, be illustrated by the examples to which we shall hereafter more particularly refer.

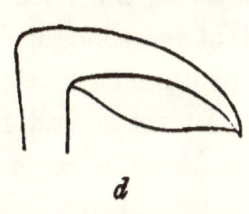

d

The entire mass of Fungi subdivide themselves naturally into two great divisions. In one of these, and by far the largest, the spores, or reproductive bodies, are naked or exposed, generally clustered in groups of four, or some multiple of that number. It will be borne in mind that in Endogenous plants, *three* is the mystical, typical, or representative number, whilst in the alliance of plants now under consideration that typical number is *four*. The first great division of fungi, in which the spores are naked, is termed SPORIFERA, or spore-bearing. In the second, or smaller division, the spores are contained in bags, or sacs, called *asci*, and the division bears the name of SPORIDIIFERA.

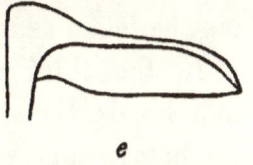

e

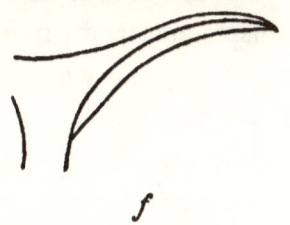

f

The *Sporiferous* division of fungi, again, contains four families, which are arranged according to the following distinctive features :—In one family, the *hymenium*, whether distributed over gills, tubes, pores, or fissures, is the most prominent object.   Hence these are called *Hymenomycetes*, a word compounded of *hymenium* and *mycetes*, the latter being the Greek term for fungi : so that these might be called *Hymenium-fungi*, of which the common mushroom may be accepted as an example.

In the second family the *hymenium* is inclosed in a *peridium*, or case, which seldom ruptures before the spores are ripe.   To this family the name of *Gastero-mycetes* is given ; from *gaster* a belly, because the hymenium, with all the reproductive bodies, are inclosed in a kind of uterus or womb, from whence they are expelled when mature.   Of this family the puff-balls may be taken as an example.

In the third family, which contains very minute individuals, the spores are the most conspicuous bodies ; the name employed is *Coniomycetes*, derived from the Greek *konis*, signifying *dust*, on account of their dust-like nature, of which mildew and smut may be taken as types.

In the fourth family the spores are small and in-conspicuous compared to the threads upon which they are borne, and which latter are the distinctive features of the family.   Hence it is termed *Hyphomycetes*, from the Greek word *hypha*, a thread ; wherefore they might be called *thread-like fungi*.   Of this family blue-mould may be taken as an example.

Having now briefly characterized the four families of Sporiferous fungi, we will return to the first of these, and examine it more minutely. .

The Hymenomycetous fungi are those in which the hymenium is the most prominent feature. In some of these the hymenium is inferior, and in some it is superior. We will commence with those in which it is inferior. This family contains six orders, of equal importance, and equally natural to similar divisions of flowering plants. It will be remembered henceforth, that we make no allusion to groups, of whatever size or importance, not represented in the " British Flora."

The first and most prominent order is termed *Agaricini*, and contains the *Gill-bearing fungi*, or those in which the hymenium, or spore-bearing surface, is inferior, and spread over lamellæ or gills, which radiate from a common centre, and each of which lamellæ may be separated into two plates.

This order is well represented in Great Britain, for we have not less than five hundred and sixty distinct species already described. The eighteen British genera will be found arranged in the systematic table appended to this volume.

The first genus of this order is often amalgamated with the second, on the authority of Fries; but Dr. Greville long ago proposed its separation. In this work we shall retain the old name of *Amanita* for the twelve species found in Britain, deeming the character of the volva to be of sufficient importance to justify their removal from the large genus with which they are often associated.

In *Amanita* the volva is distinct, the gills are membranaceous, with acute edges, and the spores are white. The volva, on breaking up, remains attached to the pileus in fragments resembling warts. Of the twelve species found in this country, many are poisonous, and one is especially deserving of notice from its extraordinary application abroad. This species, the Fly Agaric (*Amanita muscaria*), has a bright scarlet or reddish umber, pileus studded with warts of a dirty white or yellowish tint (Plate 1). The stem is bulbous, containing cottony threads. It is found most commonly in birch woods, and not very plentifully in Britain. A decoction of this fungus has been employed as a fly-poison ; whence its vulgar name.

M. Roques, in his work on Esculent Fungi, says distinctly that this plant has not its poisonous propĕrties modified by any climate. The Czar Alexis lost his life by eating of it, and yet it has been affirmed that in Kamtschatka " it is used as a frequent article of food." And we have been informed that it is cooked and eaten in Russia, albeit it is also on record that several French soldiers ate of it within the confines of the Russian dominions, and became very ill. In Siberia it supplies the inhabitants with the means of intoxication similar to that produced by the " haschisch " and " majoon " of the East. The fungi are collected during the summer months, and hung up to dry in the open air, or they are left to dry in the ground, and are collected afterwards. When the latter course is pursued, they are said to possess more powerful narcotic properties than when dried artificially. The juice of the whortleberry in

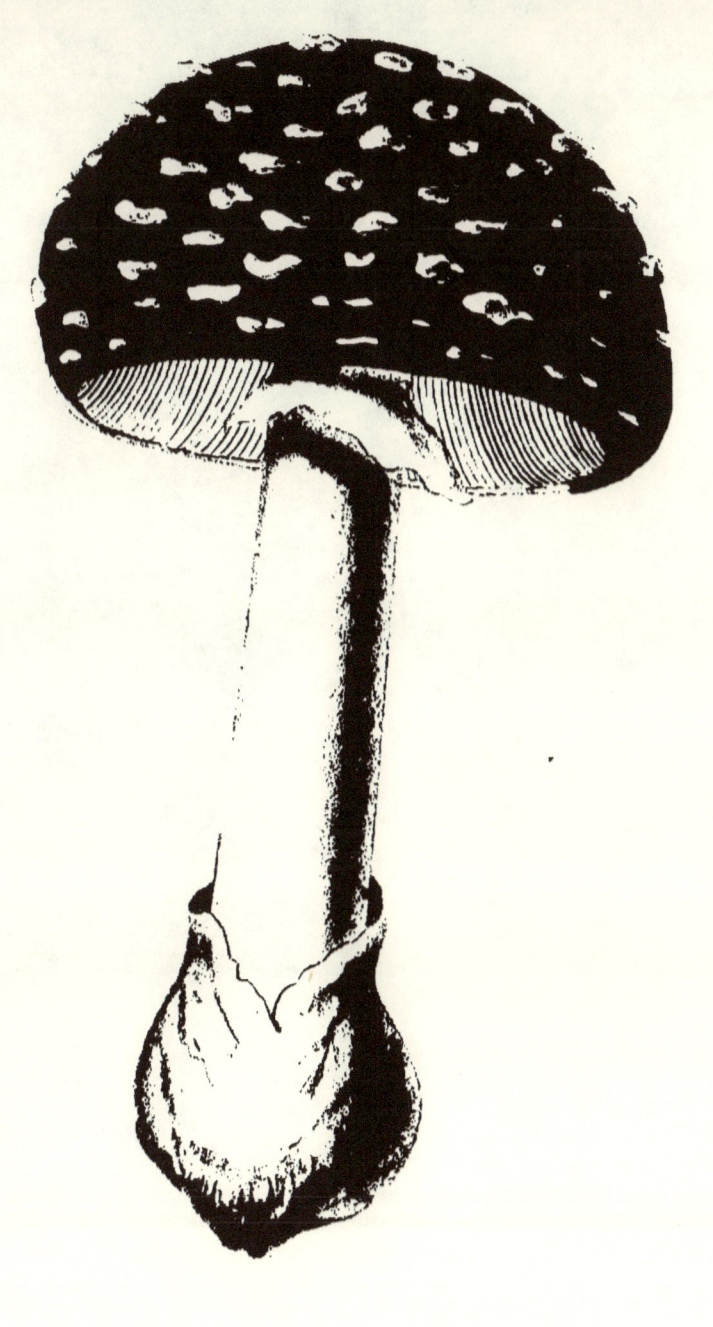

which this substance has been steeped, acquires thereby the intoxicating properties of strong wine.

The method of using this singular production is to roll it up in the form of a bolus, and swallow it whole. A day's intoxication may be procured at the expense of one or two of these fungi, and this intoxication is affirmed to be not only cheap, but remarkably pleasant. The result follows within an hour or two of participation.

Some of the effects produced by this fungus resemble those resulting from intoxicating liquors ; others are similar to the accompaniments of an indulgence in " haschisch." At first it generally produces cheerfulness, afterwards giddiness and drunkenness, ending occasionally in the entire loss of consciousness The natural inclinations of the individual become stimulated. The dancer executes a *pas d'extravagance*, the musician indulges in a song, the chatterer divulges all his secrets, the orator delivers himself of a philippic, and the mimic indulges in caricature. Erroneous impressions of size and distance are common occurrences, a straw lying in the road becomes a formidable object, to overcome which a leap is taken sufficient to clear a barrel of ale or the prostrate trunk of a British oak. But this is not the only extraordinary circumstance connected therewith. The property is imparted to the fluid excretion of rendering it intoxicating, which property it retains for a considerable time. A man, having been intoxicated on one day, and slept himself sober by the next, will, by drinking this liquor to the extent of about a cupful, become as much intoxicated as he was before. Confirmed drunkards in Siberia preserve this as a precious liquor in case a scarcity of fungi should occur. This intoxicating property may be communicated to every person who partakes of the disgusting draught, and thus with the third, fourth, and even fifth distillation. By this means, with a few fungi to commence with, a party may shut themselves in their room and indulge in a week's debauch.*

A species of *Amanita* (*A. strobiliformis*, Fr.), rarely found on the borders of woods, and which attains a large size, is said to be esculent, but is too rare to become of any importance as an article of food. The pileus is studded with persistent warts, as in the Fly Amanita; but instead of the bright red colour of that species, in this instance the pileus is of a purplish grey.

The Red Amanita (*A. rubescens*, Pers.) is also generally described as an esculent species. The whole plant becomes red when bruised or rubbed, a characteristic by which it may be readily distinguished. It is very common in woods, and has the pileus covered with scattered mealy warts. Dr. Badham and M. Roques include this amongst esculent species, and I am assured by a friend in the country, who experiments upon all the reputed esculent species which fall in his way, that "this kind makes excellent ketchup." Berkeley, notwithstanding, considers it as doubtful.

There is yet one other species of *Amanita* (*A. vagi-*

* Further details may be found in "The Seven Sisters of Sleep," by M. C. Cooke, pp. 336—345. London: James Blackwood.

nata) which is very common in woods and under
trees. It is extremely variable in size and in colour.
The pileus is thin, at first bell-shaped, and ultimately
expands to nearly a plane surface. The stem is hollow
and the volva loose. The free gills are white in the
earlier stages of growth. This species is entirely destitute of any ring. Dr. Greville found a white variety
of this species, which he calls *A. nivalis*, growing on
the bleak summits of the loftiest Grampians, where, he
says, "it enlivens the few turfy spots which occur in
those desert regions by its symmetry and extreme
whiteness. In its young state it is completely enve-
loped in the smooth volva or wrapper, and bears a near
resemblance to a pigeon's egg, scarcely rising above the
dark moss. After bursting from its confinement, it
rapidly advances to maturity, uninjured by the coldest
winds, or the snow with which it is sometimes covered,
even in the middle of August." This species has not
only enjoyed the reputation of being esculent, but also
of being poisonous. From the very questionable company
in which the three species of *Amanita* now named
are found, and from the conflicting testimony as to
their wholesome properties, we conclude that it would
be much safer to regard all the species which are
grouped under that name as suspicious, and not to
collect and employ any species of *Amanita* as an
article of food.

TRUE AGARICS.

THE genus *Agaricus* bears a name, the origin of which is involved in a little obscurity, from whence the Rev. M. J. Berkeley, the prince of British mycologists, has thus endeavoured to rescue it :—

"In all books which profess to give the derivations of botanical terms, it is said that Agaricus derives its name from Agaria, a region in Sarmatia, or from Agarus, a town and river in the same country. This derivation, at first sight, seems equally absurd with the parallel drawn by Fluellen between Macedon and Monmouth. What has Sarmatia to do with toadstools more than any other country, as they are found everywhere? The fact, however, is, that the original name, *Agaricum*, for so it stands in Pliny, had nothing whatever to do with them, but was applied by Dioscorides to a peculiar drug, supplied by the *Polyporus* of the larch, which was obtained principally, if not solely, from Agaria, but which, though formerly of considerable repute, appears now to have gone almost entirely out of use in regular practice. It is, however, still to be had of the herbalists, who import it from Germany, a form on *Larix siberica* being obtained occasionally from Archangel. As the true species occurs only on the larch, and, indeed, upon very old trees, it is confined almost entirely to places where that genus of conifers is indigenous.

"Other Polypori have often been substituted for that of the larch, and, therefore, the name *Agaricum*, or *Agaricus*, as it was afterwards written, became, to a certain extent, generic for Polyporus, and it is so used by Micheli, Ray, and others, the word *Fungus* being generally applied to what, after Linnæus, we now call Agaricus. It is to be regretted, that when that great author reformed the system of botany, he too often took any names which offered themselves in the older authors, without giving himself the trouble to inquire whether they belonged really to the plants to which they were attributed, and thus the familiar name of Agaric is now applied to plants which should never have borne it. Our earlier herbalists rightly applied it to corky arboreous fungi ; as Agaric of the oak, &c. In like manner the Greek *Hydnum*, instead of being a conspicuous pileate fungus, such as we now recognize under the name, was originally a kind of truffle ; and many other instances of similar misnomers might be adduced. It is, however, now too late to mend such matters, and we may be glad to substitute such a word as Agaric for Toadstool, which is not only disgusting in its real etymology, but helps to keep up the feeling of contempt with which a most interesting class of plants is too frequently regarded."

The *Agarics* constituting such a large and important genus, it has been found convenient to arrange them in five very natural series, according to the colour of the spores. In the first series, termed *Leucospori*, the spores are white ; of which *Agaricus procerus* may be taken as an example. In the second series, called *Hyporhodii*, the spores are salmon-coloured ; of which *Agari-*

cus prunulus will serve as an example. In the third series, denominated *Dermini,* the spores are ferruginous, and sometimes tawny or brownish ; of this series *Agaricus mutabilis* will afford a type. In the fourth series, called *Pratellæ,* in which the spores are brownish-purple or brown, the common mushroom, *Agaricus campestris,* is included. And of the fifth series, styled *Coprinarius,* in which the spores are black, we have an example in *Agaricus campanulatus.*

Each one of these series contains a number of sub-genera, which were formerly considered to have the value of genera, but which are now merely retained to serve as guides to the synonyms of old authors, or to facilitate the grouping and arrangement of species. In this work they will all be considered as species of the one genus *Agaricus.*

Under the vague and general name of mushrooms several species of fungi are consumed as articles of food. It may be true that in some localities only one or two species are dignified with the appellation of mushroom, whilst all the rest which resemble it in form are condemned as toadstools ; yet we believe that there is in prospect an age when more of those which are really worthy will be admitted to the tables of rich and poor, without that accompaniment of suspicion and dread which attaches to the dish of mushrooms. We accord perfect justice to *Agaricus campestris,* the mushroom of cultivation, whilst more delicious kinds, and equally harmless, are allowed to flourish and decay year by year without molestation.

Whoever has read Dr. Badham's "Esculent Funguses of Great Britain" will not fail to recognize the following observations :—"I have this autumn myself witnessed whole hundredweights of rich wholesome diet rotting under trees ; woods teeming with food and not one hand to gather it ; and this perhaps in the midst of potato-blights, poverty, and all manner of privations, and public prayers against imminent famine. I have, indeed, grieved when I have considered the straitened condition of the lower orders this year, to see pounds innumerable of extempore beefsteaks growing on our oaks in the shape of *Fistulina hepatica; Agaricus fusipes*, to pickle, in clusters under them ; Puffballs, which some of our friends have not inaptly compared to sweetbread, for the rich delicacy of their unassisted flavour ; *Hydna* as good as oysters, which they somewhat resemble in taste ; *Agaricus deliciosus*, reminding us of tender lamb kidney ; the beautiful Yellow Chantarelle, that *Kalon Kagathon* of diet, growing by the bushel, and no basket but our own to pick up a few specimens in our way ; the sweet nutty *Boletus*, in vain calling himself *edulis*, where there was none to believe him ; the dainty Orcella, the *Agaricus heterophyllus*, which tastes like the craw-fish when grilled ; the red and green species of *Agaricus* to cook in any way, and equally good in all." The faithful, remembrance and wholesome dread of poison lurking beneath the cap of fungi, which have filled up pages in the history of the past, mixed up with a little romance and superstition, have combined to prevent the accordance of justice to this numerous alliance of plants. It is true also that the odour and appearance of some species are repulsive enough to have warranted their association with that despised reptile which has been said to carry a jewel in its head, and with a contemptuous epithet the toadstool has been trodden under foot without even a suspicion of its use except as a throne for a toad.

Instead of the one or two species which appear in our markets in the autumn, there are upwards of fifty which might be easily discriminated from the noxious kinds, and the majority of which are fully equal, and some perhaps superior, to any of the kinds popularly considered esculent.

Foremost in the genus *Agaricus* stands a group naturally associated together under the sub-generic name of *Lepiota*, derived from the scaly appearance of the surface of the pileus (*lepis*, Lat. a scale). The hymenophorum, or part which bears the gills, is distinct from the stem, and the veil breaks up into scales on the surface of the pileus or cap. The gills differ from those in the succeeding sub-genus in being nearly or entirely free.

Occasionally, a very suspicious-looking fungus, *Agaricus procerus*, a member of this sub-genus, is found exhibited for sale in Covent Garden market, but which is, nevertheless, very good eating. It is often several inches in diameter, and is found growing in pastures. The stem is long, hollow, and bulbous at the base, clad with closely-pressed scales. The pileus

Agaricus procerus

has a thick cuticle which breaks up into distinct scales (Pl. 2). The ring is moveable and the gills are very remote, leaving a considerable distance between them and the stem. This fungus is esteemed also in Germany, France, Italy, and Spain, where it is known locally by various names; as *parasol schwamm* in Germany, *coulemelle* in France, *bubbola maggiore* in Italy, and *cogomelos* in Spain. Although it has but little flesh, it is very savoury and of an excellent odour, and is generally cooked in oil with salt, pepper, and a little garlic, the stems being excluded. An allied species, *Agaricus rachodes*, found in shady pastures, has flesh which is mostly red when bruised. The pileus is globose in the young state, but afterwards expands and becomes depressed. The cuticle is thinner than in the last-named species, and like that, is broken up into scales. It is doubted by some whether this is really a very wholesome species; it may be eaten, and we are assured by those who have eaten them that both species are equally excellent. They will, either of them, afford a good ketchup, and, consequently, realize a good price in Covent Garden, where they appear indiscriminately.

Another and smaller species of the same sub-genus (*A. excoriatus*) has been eaten, but is not to be recommended. The cuticle is also thin, and breaks up into patches. The stem is short, hollow, and nearly white. Amateurs would do well to confine their gastronomic experiments to the first-named of these species (*A. procerus*). It is so distinct in habit and general appearance, that it would be almost impossible to mistake any unwholesome species for the true Parasol Mushroom.

The most delicate of the *Lepiotas* is one found in Northamptonshire (*A. gracilentus*). It has also a thin cuticle breaking up into scales or patches. The stem is long, hollow, and slightly bulbous ; but, unfortunately, it is too unfrequent to be of any service as a source of food. In all of the four species of *Lepiota* now named, the pileus is fleshy and scaly ; the ring is moveable ; the base of the stem more or less bulbous ; and the gills are distant from the stem.

The sub-genus *Armillaria* is a small one, and contains but one species said to be edible. The three other species found in Britain are either local or uncommon. The veil is but partial, the substance of the hymenophorum, on which the gills are arranged, is continuous with the stem, and the gills are not free as in *Lepiota*. Varieties occasionally occur from which the ring is absent, at least in some of the species, if not in all.

The very common fungus *Agaricus melleus*, which constitutes the one edible species of this sub-group (Pl. 3), is found growing in dense tufts on dead stumps. It is of a pale reddish-brown colour with a tint of yellow, and is much eaten on the Continent, though possessed of an acrid taste when raw. The pileus, when fully developed, presents a level, plane surface, clad with fibrous scales. The stem is elastic, the gills white and mealy, hooked or toothed at the end.

Reports are various as to the qualities of this species ;

C.C del.   *Agaricus melleus*   F. Cooke lith.

T Way. 3. Wellington St Strand Imp.

for, while it is affirmed to be eaten largely under the name of *Hallimasch* in Vienna, and sometimes appears in the markets of that city in enormous quantities, and one author compares its flavour to that of lamb, and recommends it to be eaten as an ingredient in stews,— Dr. Badham says it is nauseous and disagreeable, and some others, that it is economically valueless. It must be confessed that the odour is not in the least disagreeable, but rather inviting, whilst the taste is slightly acrid when raw, and pleasant enough, though deficient in aroma, when cooked.

A larger group succeeds that to which we have now alluded, bearing the sub-generic name of *Tricholoma*. The characters in this group are pretty distinct, and the species often large and imposing. The veil is absent or nearly so, or, if present, is very fugitive, and the gills have a notch or sinus behind, at the extremity next to the stem. It is extremely probable that this group does not contain a single unwholesome species, and it certainly contains several with very fair esculent properties. The whole of these, and indeed almost every species except the common mushroom, are characterized by the majority of our countrymen as "toadstools:"—

"But the mandrakes, and *toadstools*, and docks, and darnels,
Rose like the dead from their ruin'd charnels;"

or, as locally termed in the eastern counties, "toadskeps," a probable corruption of "toads-cap;" for "skep" is there held and used as a synonym for a large basket, with which mushrooms have nothing in common.

Let us hope that such names, which were originated and have been perpetuated in ignorance, will soon become obsolete.

The St. George's Mushroom (*A. gambosus*) is an early species, as it makes its appearance, growing in rings, about May or June. It has a most powerful odour, and sometimes attains a very large size. Although another and very distinct species has shared the honour of bearing the name of the patron saint of England, this is believed to be the true St. George's mushroom. To whichever of the two the genuine patronage belongs, it is said to have been first ascribed to it by the Hungarians, on account of its being the special gift of that saintly champion. Others, dissenting from so romantic an origin, declare that the name resulted simply from its making its appearance about the time of St. George's day.

If the latter be the true source of the name, the present species establishes its claim to it by flourishing in spring, whilst the pretender is an autumnal species. The pileus in this mushroom is thick and fleshy, smooth, and ultimately becomes cracked and fissured. The stem is stout and solid, and the yellowish-white gills are much crowded together. The odour of this species is so strong, both in the matured state and in the earliest stages of its growth, as to become oppressive and overpowering. Workmen employed to root them out are said to have been so overcome by the odour as to be compelled to desist. Although this cannot be considered one of the most delicate-flavoured of fungi,

Agaricus prunulus

it is nevertheless welcome at such an early period of
the year when the more desirable kinds are not to be
obtained.

Perhaps our word mushroom was derived from the
French *moucheron* or *mousseron*, by which this species
seems to have been designated on account of its growing
amongst moss. In France and Italy it is so highly
esteemed that, when dried, it will realize from twelve to
fifteen shillings per pound. Its capability of under-
going successfully the drying process, gives this species
the advantage over the common mushroom, which
some have declared it already possessed on account of
its flavour. An amateur writes of it thus:—"It is
very good broiled; but the best way of cooking it is to
bake it with a little butter, pepper, and salt, in an oven,
on a plate under a basin. A great quantity of gravy
comes out of it, mingled, in the case of a good specimen,
with osmazome, which tastes very much like the similar
brown exudation on the surface of a roast leg of mutton."

Our plate (Pl. 9) has inadvertently been named
Agaricus prunulus, which, although one of the numerous synonyms of this species, is also given to another
esculent fungus hereafter described, and which has a
greyish pileus and coloured spores.

Amongst the species occasionally sold in Covent
Garden is a common one known there by the name of
Blewits, but to botanists as *A. personatus* (Pl. 4, upper
figure). When mature it has a soft, convex, smooth,
moist pileus, with a solid, somewhat bulbous stem, tinted
with lilac. The gills are of a dirty white, and rounded

D

towards the stem. This species scarcely seems to be
known as esculent on the Continent, though it constitutes one of the very few having a marketable value in
England, where it is employed chiefly for making
ketchup. It is quite essential that this species should
be collected in dry weather, and when it is not moist
with the early dew, as it absorbs moisture very readily,
and if regard be not had to these conditions in gathering,
it will probably afterwards suffer condemnation.

Opinions vary as much as tastes differ, as to the quality
of this fungus ; but though agreeable to some when
well broiled and seasoned with sweet herbs, it has a
peculiar flavour which would not commend it to others.
It certainly does not deserve to stand in the first class of
our indigenous species, and the ketchup it affords is
poor. It has the recommendation of being readily distinguished by its violet-tinted stem, and smooth, sleek
pileus, and, did it not appear in October, when other
and better species are plentiful, might be accepted as a
substitute.

The sub-genus *Clytocybe* is also well represented in
the British Flora. The name (*klitos* a declivity, and
kube, a head) originated in the funnel-shaped pileus of
some of the species. This group differs from *Tricholoma*
in the gills not having a sinus behind, they being
attached abruptly, or tapering gradually and running
down the stem. There are several esculent species to
be found in this group, some of which we shall proceed
to notice.

One fungus especially deserving attention may often

be found in our woods, growing amongst dead leaves, although without any charms of colouring to check the rambler in his path, and cause him to stay and admire. All its charms are those which appeal to the internal sensibilities of the gastric regions. This, sometimes called the Clouded Agaric (*A. nebularis*), has generally a mouse-grey or dun-coloured pileus, scarcely four inches in diameter, supported upon a robust stem of about three inches in height. The edge of the pileus is rolled in, and the fungus has altogether a smoky appearance, as though it had been exiled from town to vegetate penitentially in the wood. The gills are dirty white, numerous, and run a little way down the stem. The flesh is thick and odour strong.

It must, moreover, not be forgotten that the spores in this species are of a snowy whiteness, so abundant as to sprinkle and whiten the surrounding grass, which will enable the novice to avoid confounding it with less useful or more noxious species with pinkish or roseate spores.

All who have tried this fungus—and it is not at all difficult to distinguish—agree that it is of a most delicate flavour, and easy of digestion.

The Fragrant Agaric (*A. odorus*) is a very beautiful little species, but far from common. In dry weather especially it exhales an odour reminding one of newmown hay or melilot. The pileus is from two to three inches in diameter, and generally of a more or less greenish tint. The gills are numerous, pale, or tinged with flesh-colour. The stem is solid and firm. It has the reputation of supplying a rather delicate dish; but failing in satisfying ourselves of its merits sufficiently to serve as a basis for its recommendation, we have not given an illustration. It does not appear to be eaten on the Continent; and although included by persons amongst edible species, Roques considers its alimentary qualities as doubtful.

A very large mushroom, called appropriately *A. giganteus*, attaining sometimes the diameter of nearly a foot, is occasionally found in woods growing in rings. The pileus is covered with a fine down, and ultimately splits or cracks; the gills are very crowded, and at first white, becoming yellowish with age. This species is affirmed to be sweet and agreeable cooked in any way; and certainly some of the individuals occasionally found are large enough to furnish any one with a meal.

A very elegant little fungus (*A. dealbatus*) is occasionally found in dense clusters on mushroom-beds, and more often on the ground in fir plantations. It is of a clear ivory whiteness, especially when young, and the upper surface of the pileus, which is depressed and ultimately cup-shaped, has a satin-like appearance. The gills are crowded, thin, and white, and the stem is fibrous, thin, and equal throughout its length. The margin of the pileus is commonly waved and folded, and the whole appearance of the plant is exceedingly elegant. In our plate (Pl. 10*a*) the lower figure represents a young specimen when the pileus is but little depressed; the upper, a portion of a group fully matured.

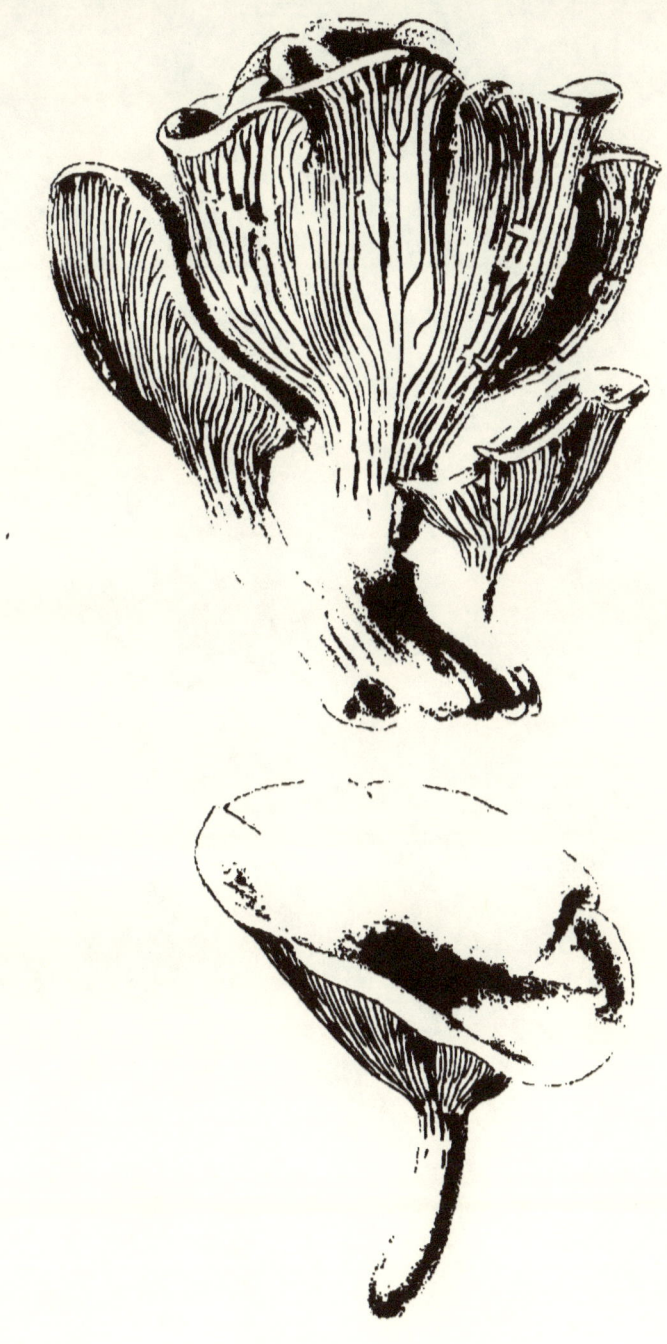

E. Cooke del et lith   Agaricus dealbatus

We can speak from recent experience of the wholesome qualities of this species. The whole substance is less watery than the common mushroom, and if old specimens are mixed in the dish, or any of them are not cooked carefully and slowly for some time, the result will prove very unsatisfactory, for they will become as tough as leather; but a dish of young individuals will make a most excellent stew, with the usual accompaniment of sweet herbs, pepper, and salt.

Another fungus (*A. geotrupus*) is often found in considerable quantities, growing in rings, in the neighbourhood of fir-trees, having a convex funnel-shaped pileus, which is either white or tan-coloured. It has a solid, compact stem, decreasing in size towards the pileus. The gills are of the colour of the pileus, crowded, and running down the stem, and have at first the odour of garlic, which afterwards resembles more that of bitter almonds. This species, especially one of its varieties, is considered excellent, equal to many, and superior to most, of our edible fungi. All the species nearly allied to it are harmless, so that there is no danger in their being confounded.

Although it is sometimes confidently affirmed that no species of fungus is good for food which grows in clusters or on old stumps, both these conditions are combined in a very common species (*A. fusipes*), which flourishes often in dense tufts in such localities, and is, moreover, very good to pickle, unless we can conceive that excellent authorities are either deceiving or deceived. This species has the pileus of a reddish-brown colour, often cracked when mature. The stem is similar in colour, tapering towards each extremity, so as to be fusiform or spindle-shaped, and generally twisted or split. The gills are nearly free, pale, and often spotted. There is considerable variation in the size and form ; but our plate represents its ordinary character (Pl. 5).

The succeeding group (*Collybia*) has also its edible representative, albeit a small one, and scarcely worthy of any eulogium. Any one who has been in the habit of noticing with any interest this singular class of plants, will have met with a very common species of this sub-genus with a rooting stem, to which the name of *A. radicatus* has been given. It is on account of this deviation in its habit from the ordinary growth of agarics that we refer to it, and not on account of any suspicion that it will ever prove valuable for any property which it may possess.

Another species of this same sub-genus, *A. velutipes*, may be found growing in tufts on old stumps long after the frosts of winter have commenced ; indeed, we have found it flourishing through the whole of the past winter, its bright yellowish cap and dark velvety stem making it an object of interest amid the desolation of this inclement season. The singular *A. tuberosus,* which is produced from little dark elongated tubers found on decaying agarics, is also a member of this sub-genus.

. The *Nagelschwamme* of the Austrian markets (*A. esculentus*) is common in the fir plantations of

M.C.C. del   *Agaricus fusipes*

Scotland, but, on account of its bitterness, is not much esteemed. It is a spring fungus, at which season large baskets of them are exposed for sale at Vienna. The pileus expands to nearly a plane surface, and is smooth and clay-coloured. The straight tough stem is of the same colour as the pileus, and the gills are loose and whitish. In size it is always small, and in quality so mediocre that one is led to wonder at its becoming a marketable commodity anywhere (Pl. 6, fig. 1).

We are not aware that the sub-genus *Mycena*, amongst its forty British species contains one that can be termed esculent. For the mycologist they possess features of interest, but none for the cook.

Of *Omphalia* our report must be to the same effect. Indeed, the species are generally so small that they can establish no claims to the honour of an experiment.

The last sub-genus of the white-spored Agarics is *Pleurotus*, or *side-foot* as some of the species have been called. This name is probably derived from two Greek words signifying *side-bone* or ribs.

The species contained in this group are lovers of wood, upon which they are generally found growing, some on living trees, others on dead stumps or posts. The stem is either inserted into the cap away from the centre or in the margin, or it is absent altogether. Some are not larger than the thumb-nail and solitary, while others are large and grow in dense masses. Some are occasionally subjected to culinary operations, but none present very great attractions to the epicure.

The trunks of elms often support a large and beautiful species, which not only makes itself a home on those venerable trees, elevated many feet above the ground, but also from them derives its specific name (*A. ulmarius*). We have seen it occasionally around Hampstead and Highgate, but it is not considered a very common species. The specimen from which our drawing was made came from the former locality ; it was flourishing alone, but it is more usual to meet with them in tufts. The stem is thick and inserted a little out of the centre ; the pileus is smooth, slightly and minutely spotted; and the gills are broad, close, and of a dirty white. Although perfectly wholesome, there is not much flavour in it, and whatever it may be when young, it certainly exhibits a tendency to toughness when fully matured, which does not recommend it to the gastronomist. It has been customary to regard this and some of its allies as alimentary, but there is no doubt that they could all be very well spared from the list (Pl. 7).

Late in the autumn the Oyster (*A. ostreatus*) may be found growing on trees. But, whilst in the animal world the oyster that groweth upon trees is considered as degenerate and unfit for becoming the food of man, in the vegetable world the tree-loving oyster is held by many to be excellent food. The fungus to which we have thus alluded has generally so peculiar an appearance, common only to a very limited number of British species, that it can scarcely be mistaken. The only one which would be liable to be confounded with it makes its appearance in spring, and is not esculent,

M C C del   *Agaricus ulmarius*

whilst the oyster is an autumnal species and is decidedly edible. The densely clustered or imbricated mass in which they are generally found, with the stems attached near the side of the pileus, the dirty white gills running far down the stem, all serve to characterize a species with which our plate (Pl. 8) can scarce fail to make one familiar. As to its value or quality when prepared for the table, there is certainly no unanimity of opinion. Another species (*A. salignus*), found sometimes solitary and sometimes in clusters on the trunks of trees, is said to be eaten in Austria, but we are not aware that it has been tried in England.

The first sub-genus in the division with salmon-coloured spores is termed *Volvaria*. The veil forms a distinct volva, and gives a decided feature to the group. One species is common in hothouses, where its satiny, dark grey cap, as it bursts and emerges from the volva, makes it an attractive object. No species is of economic importance amongst the half-dozen found in these islands.

The sub-genus *Pluteus* has the hymenophorum, or part on which the gills are situated, distinct from the stem, by which it is distinguished from the succeeding group. The veil is absent, which distinguishes it from the preceding group. There is no esculent British species.

In *Entoloma* the hymenophorum is continuous with, and the gills have a tendency to separate from, the stem.

The next sub-genus is *Clitopilus* (*klitos*, Gr., a slope, *pilos*, a cap), in which the hymenophorum is continuous with the stem, down which the attenuated gills descend in a decurrent manner. In this group we have an esculent species.

The true *A. prunulus* has the disadvantage of being often robbed of its good name. It is an autumnal species found growing in woods. The pileus is fleshy and either white or some pale shade of grey. The gills are rather distant from each other and whitish or flesh-coloured, decurrent, or running down the solid stem. The odour resembles that which one experiences on entering a flour-mill. There can be no doubt that it is a very good esculent species, but the confusion of this and *A. gambosus* under the same name has perhaps led some to attribute to it part of the honour due to its rival. In our plate the species named *A. prunulus* is the St. George's mushroom (*A. gambosus*), the latter being a vernal, and the former an autumnal species.

Three other sub-genera complete the division of Agarics in which the spores are salmon-coloured; these are, *Leptonia*, *Nolanea*, and *Eccilia*.

In *Leptonia* the stem has a cartilaginous bark. The margin of the pileus is at first curved inwards, and the gills divide away from the stem.

In *Nolanea* the stem is cartilaginous, but instead of being curved at first, the margin of the pileus is straight, and closely pressed to the stem.

In *Eccilia* the stem is also cartilaginous, and the pileus at first inflexed at the margin; the gills are attenuated behind, and truly decurrent, or running down the stem. Until very lately, it was not known that this

Agaricus ostrealus

sub-genus had a representative in Britain. One species has, however, been discovered; but in none of these sub-genera do we recognize any species that is edible.

The series called DERMINI, which have rust-coloured or tawny spores, is also divided into sub-genera, the first of which is *Pholiota*, probably derived from the Greek *pholidotos*, and signifying " covered with scales," which is a characteristic of many of the species. In this group the stem is furnished with a ring. It has been stated that *A. mutabilis*, a member of this sub-genus, is esculent; but, having great doubt of the truth of the assertion, we shall not admit it as such. Another species (*A. squarrosus*), which is commonly found growing in dense clumps on trunks of trees, with its cap and stem rough, and bristling with innumerable dark scales, has been found to be wholesome, but we have many others far more worthy of recommendation.

In this same group occurs a more commendable species (*A. pudicus*), but unfortunately it cannot be called common. The pileus is fleshy, smooth, and of a dirty white colour. The stem is solid and of the same size throughout its length. The gills are at first whitish and ultimately tawny. This fungus will be found growing on trees, more particularly on elder trunks, and has been recommended as wholesome and agreeable.

In *Hebeloma*, the veil, when present at all, is thread-like, and the gills have a sinus or depression at the extremity next the stem. Several species are very common, but none are esculent.

The sub-genus *Flammula* has the gills either firmly attached to or running down the stem.

In *Naucoria* the stem is of a cartilaginous character on the outside and the pileus or cap is bent or turned inwards. A very common little species may be noticed during the summer in almost every pasture, having a fleshy hemispherical pileus; whence its specific name of *semi-orbicularis* is derived.

In the sub-genus *Galera*, the pileus is somewhat bell-shaped, and the margin is straight.

The next sub-genus, *Crepidotus*, has an eccentric pileus, which distinguishes it from all the others. This completes the series with rust-coloured or tawny spores. It will have been remarked that in all this series there does not occur a single species which can be recommended as an article of food. Although interesting to the mycologist, our space will not permit us to give more than this brief summary of the principal features of the groups into which the series is subdivided.

Succeeding these are the PRATELLÆ, a series of Agarics in which the spores are brownish purple or brown, and the first and foremost sub-genus is *Psaliota* (from *psalion*, Gr., a ring), having the veil affixed to the stem, and forming a ring. In this group we encounter the Mushroom of the English, the Pratiola of the Italians, or the *A. campestris* of botanists (Pl. 10). "May he die of a pratiola!" is the worst wish that an Italian can express for an enemy. Hence we may learn the small esteem in which our general favourite is held by the most extensive of fungi-eaters in Europe. Were this

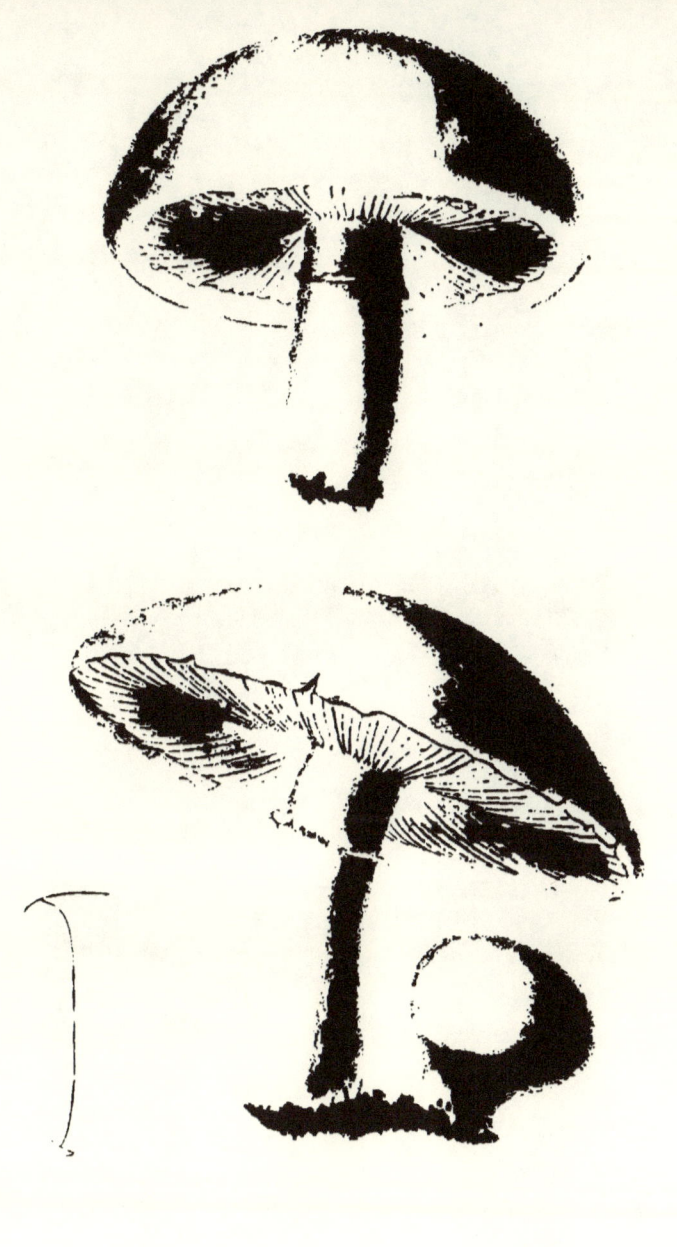

species to appear in the markets of Rome for sale, it would be certain of condemnation by the Inspector of Fungi as unwholesome. *Autres hommes, autres mœurs.* In Milan it only became recognized as worthy of being eaten after Vittadini had stood up as its champion, and in the Venetian states it is scarcely known. The suspicion that attaches to this fungus in the Peninsula extends even to Hungary, where it seldom appears at table, although the *Boletus,* so rarely eaten in England, furnishes a common dish. At Vienna, on the other hand, the rejected pratiola meets with a welcome, and is enjoyed with impunity. In France, as in Britain, it is probably the one most extensively consumed ; although in the former country the consumption of other kinds is more common than in the latter. For the true enjoyment of a mushroom, much will depend upon the method of cooking, which, notwithstanding the little variety in the methods employed here, may be served up in a number of ways. From amongst the most common of continental modes, the following are selected.

Having picked a number of freshly-gathered mushrooms, cut them in pieces, wash them in cold water, and dry them in a cloth. Put them in a pan, with butter, parsley, salt, and pepper, and place them over a brisk fire. When ready, add cream and yolk of egg, to bind them together.

Some tastes are in favour of having them dressed *à la Provençale,* in which case they must only be cut in two, washed and dried as before, and then soaked in oil for one or two hours, with salt, pepper, and a piece of garlic ; at the end of this period they should be put into a stewpan, with oil, and cooked over a brisk fire ; when done, a little chopped parsley and some lemon-juice should be added.

There is a delicacy under the form of stuffed mush-. rooms, which, although unknown to us by practical experience, is so strongly recommended by those who count them amongst their experiences, that we are induced to quote M. Roques's instructions for their preparation. " Take mushrooms of a medium size, and prepare for them at the same time the following stuffing ; *i.e.*, Take a piece of butter, grated bacon, some bread-crumbs, sweet herbs, garlic, salt, coarse pepper, and the least morsel of spice ; when these are all well mixed, turn over the mushrooms with the concave side upwards, take away the stems, and fill the concavity with this stuffing ; then wrap each in paper, and cook them in a pan, adding a spoonful of oil as occasion may require. If thought fit, a few slices of fowl, partridge, or pheasant may be added."

There is also an economical method, and one which may serve alternately with, or as a substitute for, the slovenly old English plan, which seems to reduce all cooking to three types—roast beef, boiled mutton, and grilled chops or steaks ; even mushrooms must be cooked upon one of these plans, unless we can induce a change for the better. Having peeled your mush-rooms, and removed the stems, place them in a stewpan, with fresh butter, and let them stew over a brisk fire ; when the butter is melted, squeeze in the juice of a lemon ; after a little while add salt, pepper, spice, and a spoonful of water in which a clove of garlic has been soaked for half an hour ; let them stew all together for about an hour, and then add yolk of egg to bind them ; pour your stew upon some small crusts of bread which you would have previously fried in butter.

A variety that is charming may be found on "cold-mutton days" in hashing the mutton with mushrooms, making what our transmarine neighbours would call *Hachis aux champignons.* To accomplish this, two dozen mushrooms should be selected, washed, and well dried, then put in a stewpan with a piece of butter. When the butter is melted, stir in a tablespoonful of flour, two glasses of beef gravy, salt, pepper, and a bay-leaf. These should be cooked until reduced one-half, and then poured over the hashed leg of mutton. The whole should be well mixed together, and served with small crusts of bread fried in butter.

To make a *Purée* of mushrooms, select such as are of a globular shape, called locally in some parts "button mushrooms," wash them in cold water, and wipe them dry : chop them as fine as possible, and press them in a cloth ; put them in a stewpan, with a little butter and pepper, let them stand over a brisk fire, and when the butter is melted, squeeze in lemon-juice, and add jelly-broth, according to the quantity of mushrooms ; stew until reduced to the consistency of pea-soup, and serve with meat, fish, or poached eggs.

These recipes will suffice to show that there are more ways of cooking mushrooms than stewing them indefinitely in an uncertain quantity of water, or committing them to the gridiron "*sans* everything." It will not be necessary to append a description of a species so well known ; but it may not be out of place to repeat the recommendation, that to retain all their aroma, as well as to prevent any unpleasant consequences from a free indulgence in them, care should be taken to reject such as have lost by age the pinkish tint of the gills, and to cook those selected as speedily as possible after being gathered.

The varieties into which this fungus diverges are almost infinite ; both the cultivated and uncultivated kinds presenting great deviations from typical forms, as great, indeed, as in some instances separate species, and as such some authors have regarded them.

The cultivation of mushrooms has not hitherto received attention equal to that which has been bestowed upon other garden vegetables, and all the attention which they have received is centred in this one species, as far as English horticulturists are concerned. The promoters of a well-known journal devoted to practical horticulture have once and again recommended experiments on other species, but apparently hitherto with but little success. It may be, that while there are prizes offered for fine cauliflowers or rich grapes, there are none for "improved mushrooms."

A kind of mushroom is found in meadows, growing in large rings, and often attaining an enormous size, which has been considered by some as only a variety of the common mushroom, and by others as a distinct species (*Agaricus arvensis*, Schœff,). The name of St. George (*Agaricus Georgii*) has been applied to this, as well as to another species of *Agaricus*. Locally it is sometimes called the horse-mushroom, from its size, and one variety is termed "Springers." The gills are at first paler, and when old, of a darker brown than those of the pasture-mushroom. They are said to be coarser and less finely-flavoured, but to make excellent ketchup, for which purpose they are occasionally sold. Like its ally, the common mushroom, it has several varieties, and some of these are of a much finer flavour than others. To some palates the taste of this species is affirmed to be more agreeable than that of the other. It is worthy of consideration whether some of these varieties might not be cultivated, and, perhaps, thereby improved, as well as the ordinary bed-mushroom, which is probably not the very best which could have been selected for the purpose.

There are no other examples of edible species to be found in the remaining sub-genera of the PRATELLÆ, or brownish-spored series. In *Hypholoma* the veil is web-like, adhering to the pileus at the margin. During the autumn nearly every post or old stump has its base adorned with clusters of a yellow fungus, with greenish-grey gills. It is very variable in size, and at times much contorted in form; but so common is it, and so readily recognized, that we are almost tempted to regret that, not only is it bitter and unpleasant to the taste, but probably dangerous. This species, which is named *A. fascicularis*, from its habit of growing

E

in fascicles or bundles, belongs to the sub-genus *Hypholoma*.

The next sub-genus, *Psilocybe*, is sometimes without a veil, and when present it is not in the form of a ring, which also characterizes the succeeding sub-genus, from which this may be known by the pileus having its margin at first curved inwards; whilst in *Psathyra* the margin is at first straight.

The last series of true Agarics, in which the spores are black (*Coprinarii*), is a small one with but two sub-genera, *Panæolus* and *Psathyrella*. In the former the veil is interwoven, the pileus is inclined to be fleshy, with the margin extending beyond the gills. In the latter the veil is not interwoven, and the pileus is thin, with its margin not extending beyond the gills. The members of the first sub-genus are found on dung, and of the last under hedges. They are all so small, that no one would think of committing them to the charge of the cook for the sake of experiment.

PSEUDO-AGARICS.

CLOSELY associated with the last sub-genus of the genus *Agaricus*, and agreeing therewith in some points, is the genus *Coprinus*, which differs mainly in the deliquescent character of its membrane-like gills. The spores are black, as in *Coprinarius*; therefore it is to the melting or deliquescing gills that the attention must be directed.

In almost every rich pasture, and often in gardens,

M.C.C del   *Coprinus comatus*

we meet, during the autumn, with the Maned Agaric (*Coprinus comatus*), commanding attention by its singular and graceful form. It rises from the ground like a cylinder with a rounded end, and afterwards the cap opens to the size and shape of a hand-bell. The whole surface is delicate and silky, and the cap, tinged with brown at the top and greyish at the base, soon becomes covered with scales as of entangled threads. The stem is of a glossy unsullied whiteness, tall, tapering upwards, and hollow within. The narrow ring which surrounds the stem is seldom fixed. The gills are very close together, and are at first pinkish, passing through shades of purple and brown to black. The substance of the hymenophorum, or that portion of the pileus on which the gills are situated, is very thin, and soon becomes torn and split at the margin. In this state probably its name originated (*coma*, a wig), for it bears a fancied resemblance to a wig upon a barber's block. This species is so rapidly deliquescent, that while standing, or more speedily if gathered, it melts away drop by drop, and is soon converted into a black fluid resembling ink; and indeed this resemblance is so complete, that it may readily be employed as a substitute; all that is required being to boil and strain it, and add a small quantity of corrosive sublimate to prevent its turning mouldy. There is generally no difficulty in procuring them for this or any other purpose at the proper season. During the past autumn they have been exceedingly abundant in some places, especially in the gardens of Chelsea Hospital. If gathered young, they afford no despicable dish, though perhaps not quite equal to the common mushroom. Even when more advanced, they may be converted into a very passable ketchup. This condiment will then be equal to the majority of samples sold as mushroom ketchup, made too often from a very heterogeneous mixture of species, and not always before these have passed into a state of decomposition. Whether prepared for the table or for ketchup, it should always be remembered that the sooner the preparation takes place after the fungi are gathered the better. The plants have been blamed "many a time and oft" for being unwholesome, or affording an indifferent ketchup, when the blame ought to have rested in the kitchen. (Pl. 11.)

Closely allied to the Maned Agaric is another species (*Coprinus atramentarius*) greatly resembling it in appearance, except that the scales are absent from the pileus, which in this instance is smooth and of a greyish colour. It is extremely common about old stumps and also in gardens, flourishing on the naked soil. This species is often found in large clusters, and for all esculent purposes should be collected young. It has not only a similar habit, but also similar properties to the foregoing. When fully expanded and melting away in inky drops, it is unfit for anything except to replenish the inkstand. Popular prejudice is as strong against fungi of this kind as against the gigantic frondose polypori and the puff-ball, and one might almost as readily hope to convince the labourer in agricultural districts that flint stones are convertible into soup as

Coprinus atramentarius

that such "toad's meat" are fit for the table of a Christian. (Pl. 12.)

The genus *Bolbitius* is small and unimportant, but that of *Cortinarius*, which succeeds it, must not be so speedily dismissed. In this genus, while the gills are membranaceous as in *Coprinus*, they do not deliquesce, or melt away. The veil consists of threads of an arachnoid, or spider's web texture, and the spores are commonly of the colour of rust of iron. This genus is subdivided into six groups, founded on minor distinctions, and the names are given in the tabular arrangement at the end of this volume.

One of the brightest and most beautiful of this, or any other British genus, not only commends itself to our notice on this account, but also for its excellence as food. The species to which we allude (*Cortinarius violaceus*) is found in woods, although by no means common. The colour is a beautiful dark violet, sometimes approaching nearly to black, with a coppery-red gloss or shade. The stem is bulbous and spongy, with a white cottony substance at the base. The gills are broad, thick, and distant; and the spores are of a rusty brown. There is such a distinctness about the character of this species that one regrets it is not more common, especially when we remember that it has not only the taste and odour of the mushroom when raw, but it is of "a particularly rich flavour when cooked." M. Roques states that he has eaten it, and does not hesitate to include it amongst those of good quality.

The *Marron* of the French, and *Cortinarius casta-*

neus of botanists, is only a small species deriving both
its French and its scientific name from its chestnut
colour.   It is common in woods and gardens on the
naked ground, and has violet stem and gills, the latter
becoming ultimately of a rusty brown.   It is certainly
a wholesome esculent species, but a great number would
be required to make a good dish.

The Cinnamon Mushroom (*C. cinnamomeus*) is a very
common species, with a cinnamon-coloured pileus and a
yellowish flesh.   It is a lover of woods, and in northern
latitudes is found inhabiting them everywhere.   In its
fresh state it has the odour and flavour of the spice
after which it is named, so powerful and peculiar to
itself, that this alone is a good test of its identity.
The Germans are said to be very fond of this species,
which is generally stewed in butter and served with
sance for vegetables.

The small genera *Paxillus* and *Gomphidius* are
intermediate between *Cortinarius* and *Hygrophorus*.
In this latter genus the main feature is found in the
waxy character of the hymenium or spore-bearing
surface.

Herein are found three species, more or less available
for culinary purposes.   The best of these (*H. virgineus*)
is of a beautiful, pure ivory whiteness when in good
condition, becoming dingy or tawny when old.   The
gills are distant and decurrent, or produced down the
stem.   It is common on short pastures and downs, and
although small is well worth the trouble of collecting.   Without a continental reputation, although

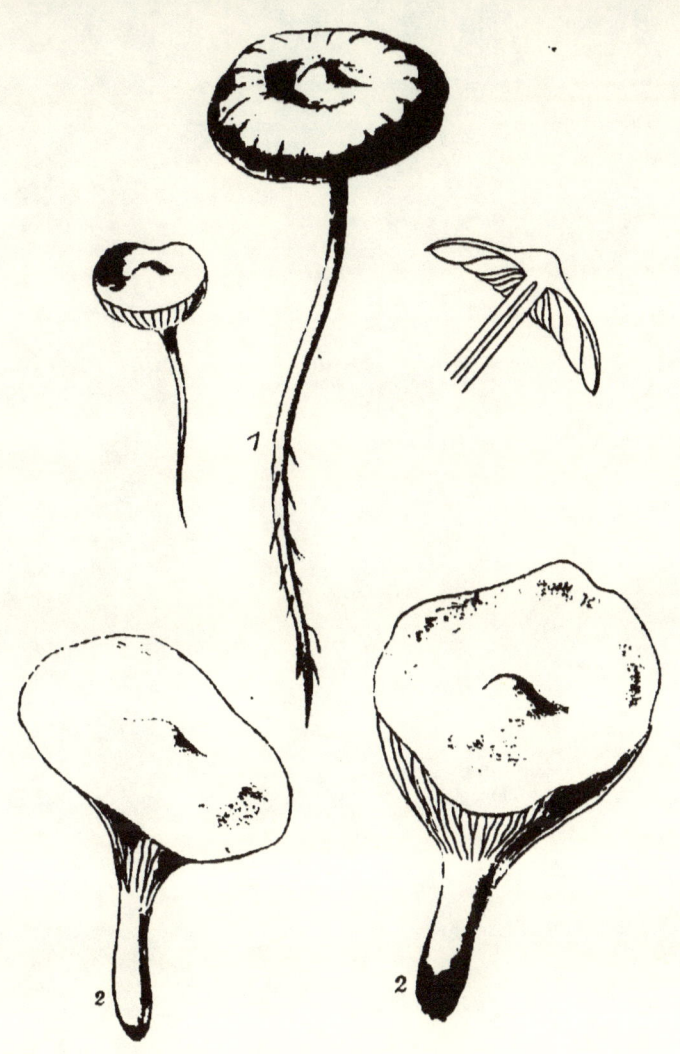

1 Agaricus esculentus
2 Hygrophorus virgineus

E Cooke lith

occasionally eaten in France, it merits a better acquaintance. When cooked, the method recommended is to stew them gently with fine herbs and delicate sauce : in this manner, Berkeley says that they may supply the place of better species, and a correspondent who always economizes all he meets with affirms that they are excellent. It is believed that our figures (Pl. 6, fig. 2) will enable the amateur to distinguish them with facility.

The second species (*H. pratensis*) is found in open pastures in the autumn, not uncommonly. In colour it is variable, in all shades between a light buff and a dark orange. Its habits are gregarious, growing generally in tufts and sometimes in parts of circles. The pileus is slightly elevated in the centre, and smooth. The stem becomes rather smaller at the base, and is more or less spongy in the interior. The gills are not numerous, but thick and decurrent, and of a reddish buff-colour, and there is no trace of a ring. In colour, therefore, it is readily distinguished from the last species, although occasionally it may be found nearly white. In habit and general appearance it resembles *H. virgineus*. It is perfectly wholesome, and is sometimes eaten in France; and if not quite equal to the other, it is certainly preferable to some which have been more strongly recommended. It is scarcely necessary to caution our readers against an allied species of the same genus, which is extremely variable in colour, and is at first covered with a greenish evanescent gluten. The best that can be said of it is that it is suspicious.

It is sometimes called the Parrakeet Mushroom (*H. psittacinus*), and its tints are generally bright, combining parrot-like hues; whence its cognomen has been derived.

The third edible species (*H. eburneus*) cannot be so well recommended as either of the others, to the first of which it bears some resemblance, but may be distinguished from it by the glandular scales with which the upper portion of the stem is dotted. This is also common, but prefers woody localities, and betrays a foxy tint as it decays. Did it not flourish in a different situation, there would at least be no dangerous results from confounding the species.

To these might be added still another species (*H. niveus*), which so nearly resembles *H. virgineus* that it may not ultimately prove to be specifically distinct from it. It is, moreover, much smaller, being sometimes so insignificant that it would appear absurd to talk of cooking it, notwithstanding that it is very common in pastures. Whenever found large enough, it may be eaten with *H. virgineus*, from which the amateur will find a difficulty in distinguishing it.

The group of Agarics now classed together as a genus under the name of *Lactarius*, are distinguished by the presence of a milky fluid, from whence the generic name has been derived. This fluid is commonly at first white, but in one instance it is coloured. In certain of the British species this milk is acrid, and the fungi of that group are not only valueless as food, but many of them are decidedly injurious. There are but two out of nearly thirty species which can be recommended

Cantharelius abarius. 1.
Lactarius deliciosus 2.

with any confidence, and even these have not escaped the censure of some who perhaps have never tested them. In France they appear to be held in but little repute, although in other continental countries they are sought after and esteemed. In Austria, for example, they are considered equal to any that are brought to table.

One would imagine from the name (*Lactarius deliciosus*) given to the reddish orange fungus found in almost every fir plantation, that it would be a treasure to an epicure ; and so indeed it is, if the testimony of Sir James Smith is to be received, that "it really deserves its name, being the most delicious mushroom known.". A gentleman of our acquaintance says that whenever he finds them he considers himself possessed of the greatest treat which the fungoid world has to offer ; but that, having made their virtues known to his neighbours, it is now but seldom that he has the good fortune to enjoy them. (Pl. 13, lower figure.)

The pileus in this species is fleshy, and depressed in the centre, of a reddish orange, with zones or rings of a darker colour ; the stem and gills are also of an orange colour. The milk which it contains is at first of a deep yellow, but upon exposure turns to a dull green : when raw, the taste is slightly acrid. In some seasons and in some localities this species is very common, especially in the fir plantations of Scotland ; and the characters are so distinct that there is no fear of mistaking any other species for it.

The other esculent species (*Lactarius volemum*) is

not common. When found, it generally occurs in woods, and will attain a diameter of four inches. It is of a golden tawny colour, and the crowded gills, which are at first white, become ultimately yellowish. The milk in this species is abundant and white, wherein it differs from the preceding. There is a more common species of *Lactarius*, found generally in fir plantations, with a darker coloured reddish pileus and white milk; but it is acrid and disagreeable to the taste, whereas the milk of *L. volemum* is mild.

It would be well to guard carefully against the red species, as it is certainly dangerous; and should the colour not be sufficiently decided to satisfy the collector, the taste will at once set the matter at rest. · If the reader has ever inadvertently masticated the leaf, or a portion of the root of that common hedge-side plant called locally " Lords and Ladies " (*Arum maculatum*), he will have experienced some such a sensation as would have resulted from the mastication of a portion of one of the acrid milky fungi to which we have alluded.

Lactarius volemum has been celebrated from the earliest times, and when properly prepared is said to resemble lamb's kidney. The method employed is to mince as many as may be required and fry them in a pan with a piece of butter, stirring them about meanwhile : when done, strew over them salt and pepper, parsley chopped fine, a small portion of shalot, and a little flour. Add, finally, a glass of champagne (or perry will answer nearly as well), and a little of the juice of a lemon, and cayenne.

The genus *Russula* may be known from the last by the stiff, sharp-edged gills not being milky. It contains some of the best and some of the worst of fungi, viewed in an alimentary aspect, and some of the most brilliantly coloured of British species. There is evidence of the little interest which fungi have hitherto possessed in the popular mind, in the general absence of vulgar or local names for the different species. This may in part be accounted for in the similarity of external form in many of the Agarics, but other causes have had their influence. A mushroom, a toadstool, and a puffball in many districts will comprise the entire vocabulary for the larger kinds. Had they been pleasant to the eye, agreeable to the nose, or of reputed miraculous power in curing the ills that flesh is heir to, each would have enjoyed a cognomen by which it would have been recognized as readily as the dandelion or daisy, heartsease or violet. Returning, however, to *Russula*, which we cannot characterize by a more popular name. Of two species found in woods which are deserving of notice, one (*R. vesca*) is far from common, and the characters are scarcely such as could be described without fear of mistake on the part of the unscientific, or those to whom the plant is hitherto unknown. Had our space permitted of the introduction of a figure, some of these difficulties would doubtless have vanished.

The other species (*R. heterophylla*), though very variable in colour, is so common and well known, at least by sight, if not by name, that, with our figure (Pl. 4, lower figure) before us, we will venture a

description.   The pileus is firm and fleshy, ultimately
becoming depressed, often of some shade of grey.   The
gills are white, much crowded together, and forked.
The stem is white, solid, and firm.

Both these species are covered in their young state
with a thin pellicle, or superficial skin, which disappears
with age, and the latter especially is subject to great
variations in colour.

Another mild species (*R. lepida*), not very common,
may be met with in the Kentish woods and elsewhere.
It has a compact, fleshy pileus, with a solid white
or pinkish stem, and rounded, thickish, white gills,
crowded together.   It is commonly consumed on the
Continent, where it is much more plentiful than with
us.

A species (*R. virescens*) with a rough, warty, greenish
pileus, is occasionally found in woods.   It has also a
whitish stem and gills, but, although very wholesome,
it is not common enough to be of importance as a food
resource.   In France this species is said to be preferred
by some to the ordinary mushroom, and is known in
the south under the name of "Verdette."   It is common in Languedoc, where it is collected and grilled
with small herbs and oil.

There is, however, a very common species (*R. aluta-
cea*) found in similar localities, which, like all the other
edible species of *Russula*, is mild to the taste when
raw.   The pileus is generally depressed and changeable
in colour.   The stem is stout, and either white or red.
The gills are always yellowish in all stages of growth.

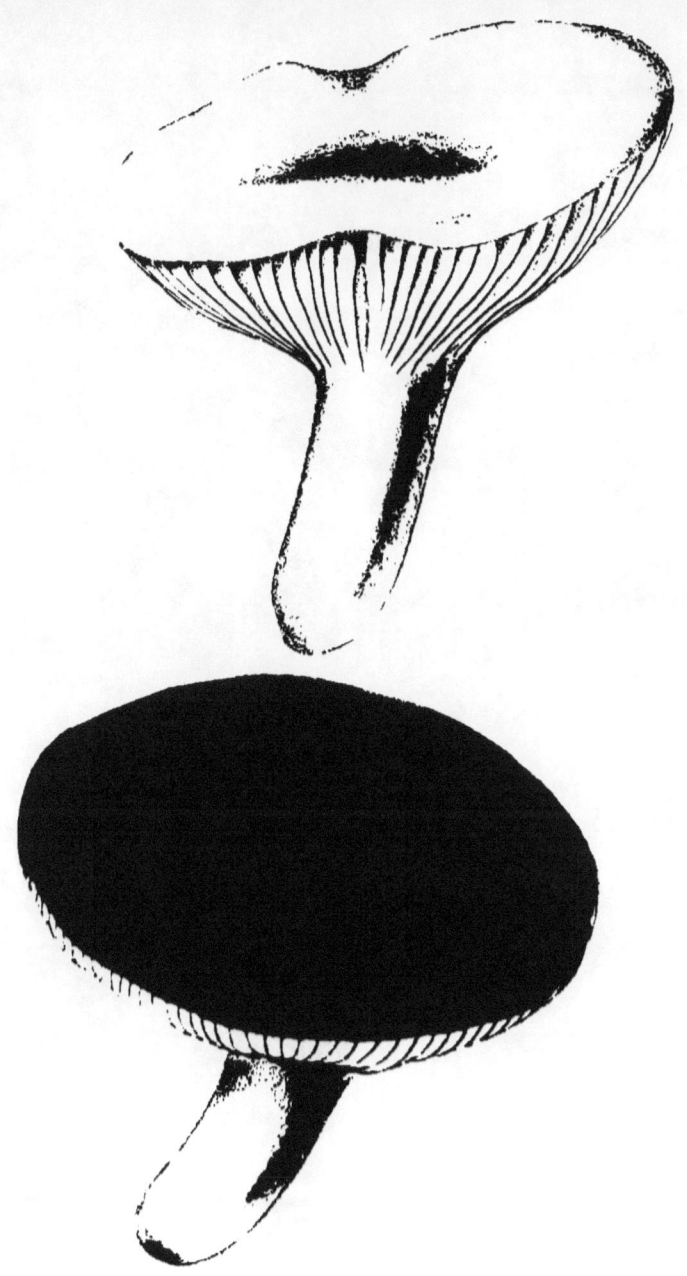

Russula emetica

The large size and yellowish gills are sufficient to distinguish this species from all its congeners. Its flesh is soft and savoury, and may be eaten without fear of unpleasant consequences.

We have already hinted at the poisonous character of some members of this genus. As an example we might refer to one which fortunately is not very common with us (*R. emetica*), and which, could we forget· its character, would commend itself by the beauty of its colours and the variety of their shades. Although red is by far the most common tint, this sometimes fades into pink, or deepens into purple. The surface of the pileus is smooth and shining, and the flesh beneath—as well as the broad gills and solid stem—white. Many are the stories of disasters recorded from the inadvertent indulgence in the Emetic Agaric, as it is sometimes termed, only a small fragment of which is said to occasion unpleasant sensations, and establish its claims to its specific name. It is questionable whether any amount of culinary preparation will remove all its poisonous properties, notwithstanding that the acrid juices of many plants are of so volatile a nature that they may often be dispelled by heat, as in the case of the root of the Mandioca plant of Brazil, from whence tapioca is prepared. Two figures of this species are given in our plate (Pl. 22), which represent the shades of colour in the pileus most usually encountered.

There are also two or three other members of this genus believed to be equally dangerous, and perhaps more common ; so that, under all circumstances, it would be more advisable to reject all than risk any, unless the esculent species are so well known that there is not the remotest possibility of a poisonous species associating with its betters unawares. This advice is given in remembrance of the fact that the poison of the dangerous species is so powerful that a single specimen is capable of producing most unpleasant and fatal results.

The genus *Cantharellus* has thick, swollen, and branched gills, with the edges blunt and rounded so as to have the appearance of veins rather than gills.

The beautiful little yellow Chantarelle (*Cantharellus cibarius*) having been once seen, is sure to be recognized, and, once tasted, to be remembered. It is of a bright, deep yellow colour, with a smell like that of ripe apricots ; the pileus becomes at first convex and afterwards funnel-shaped. (Pl. 13, upper figure.) The gills are thick and branched, and of the same colour as the pileus. The chantarelle is common in woods and occasionally in more open localities, although another species unworthy of commendation is generally found on heaths and commons.

Berkeley states that "the chantarelle is occasionally served up at public dinners at the principal hotels in London on state occasions, where every effort is made to secure the rarest and most costly dainties." In some parts of Kent, and also in Sussex, they may be found in profusion at the proper season of the year, and there is no reason why their use should be confined to first-class hotels and "state occasions" provided the preju-

dice against eating "toadstools" could be overcome.
Persons who do not emulate French cookery, or cannot
provide the adjuncts, are recommended to prepare the
chantarelle as they would the common mushroom;
taking care that their stew is not hurried, for if boiled
too violently they might as soon experiment upon shoe-
makers' parings, for their chantarelles will become " as
tough as leather." In France, Germany, Austria, and
Italy, this fungus is alike esteemed, and it is not at
all uncommon to hear from epicures who have been
fortunate enough to encounter a well-cooked dish of
chantarelles, rapturous encomiums on this golden
fungus.

Batarra says that if properly prepared the chantarelle
would arrest the pangs of death. But regardless of
what Batarra or Trattinick, Roques or Vittadini may
say, we would advise our readers to taste and try for
themselves, should a dish of chantarelles ever come in
their way. To this end we will give directions for
cooking them, as employed in France.

After having picked and washed them, they are put
into boiling water, then stewed in fresh butter, a little
olive oil, chopped tarragon, pepper, salt, and a little lemon-
peel : when they are cooked, they are allowed to gently
simmer over a slow fire for fifteen or twenty minutes,
and moistened from time to time with beef gravy or
cream : when about to be served, the stew is thickened
with yolk of egg.

As a substitute for such elaborate cookery the chantarelles may be simply fried in butter or oil, with

pepper and salt, adding a few bread-crumbs, or pouring them when done over a slice of toasted bread.

The chantarelle may be preserved for winter use, either by drying in a current of air, or pickling in salt and water, and before being used, soaked a short time in lukewarm water.

The genus *Nyctalis*, which is intermediate between the last and the next, contains species which are small in size and parasitic in habit, and of which we have but two representatives.

In *Marasmius*, the hymenophorum, or part which bears the gills, though continuous with the stem, is different in texture. The spore-bearing surface is dry, and the folds are thick and tough, but sharp or acute at the edge. The majority of species are also rather small in size, but are not parasitic on other fungi, as in the last genus.

It is a singular fact that whilst in this country "mushroom" is a kind of general name for all the edible species, in France its synonym "mousseron" is applied to but one species, whilst "champignon," which is used in the latter country as a general term for all fungi, is in England restricted to one species, which is a member of the present genus.

The little Fairy-ring Champignon (*Marasmius oreades*) is one of the privileged few that enjoy a good reputation; but even in this instance the reputation is but local. (Pl. 14, upper figure.) In the dried state they are available for culinary purposes, whilst thousands of them annually rot on the pastures where

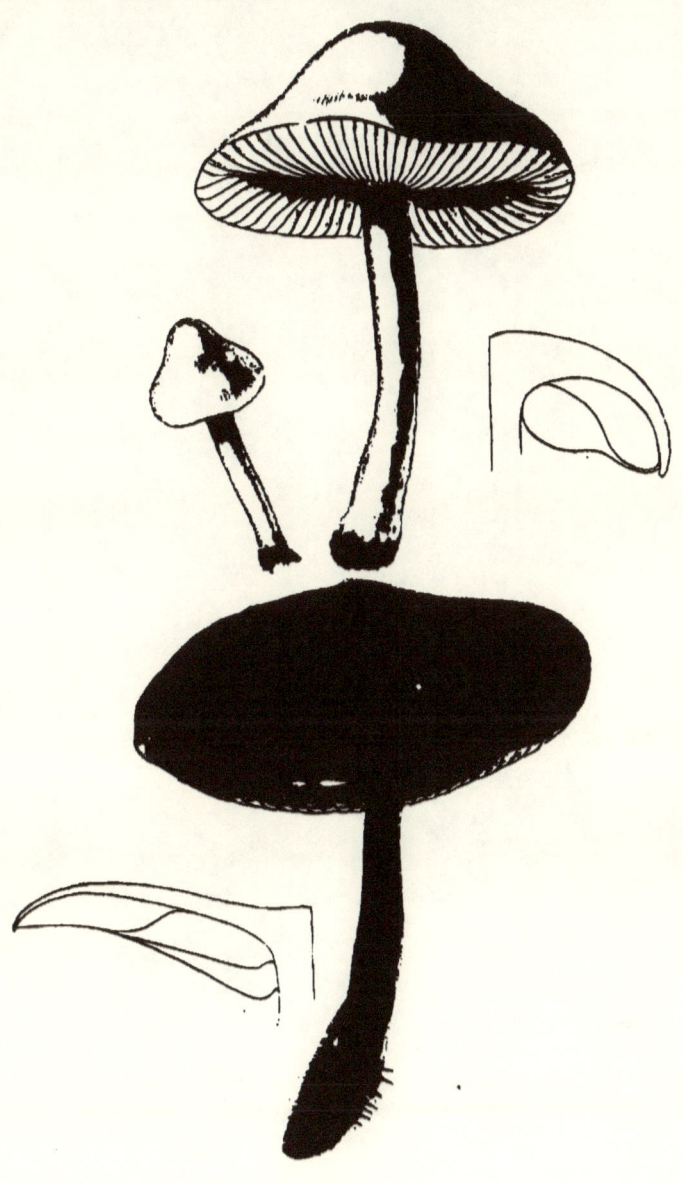

Marasmius   oreades

Marasmius   peronatus   *E. Cooke. lith.*

they grow without a hand to gather them. There is very little difficulty in recognizing the champignon, which is found growing in rings, and the pileus at first is of a brownish ochre, becoming paler as it grows older, until it fades into a rich cream-colour. Another species is occasionally found mixed with it, which might perhaps by carelessness be mistaken for it, but not if the two are compared. The taste of *Marasmius urens*, the latter species, is acrid, and the gills yellowish or brownish, and narrower than in the true champignon: the stem of both is alike solid, but in the spurious kind clothed with a white down at the base, whilst in the edible kind it is quite naked. A third allied species (*Marasmius peronatus*) is some times found in woods, but this is generally larger, and has the' base of the stem clothed with yellow stiff hairs or bristles. (Pl. 14, lower figure.) As we should not search for the true champignon in' woods, there is less fear of mistaking this species. There is scarcely a more delicious fungus than the champignon, and the chance of confounding other species with it is more imaginary than real. The evidence of the Rev. M. J. Berkeley is strongly in its favour:—" When of a good size and quickly grown, it is perhaps the best of all fungi for the table, whether carefully fried or stewed with an admixture of finely-minced herbs and a minute portion of garlic. It is at the same time tender and easy of digestion, and when once its use is known and its characters ascertained, no species may be used with less fear. It is so common in some districts that bushels

F

may be gathered in a day." They may also be readily dried by stringing the caps together on a thread and suspending them in a dry kitchen, and when thoroughly dried may be kept in close tins. Only a month or two since the same gentleman, whose name we have already mentioned, directed attention to this species in the pages of the *Gardeners' Chronicle*, in terms of strong commendation. Indeed, we could not mention a species the evidence in whose favour is so strong, and yet bushels are allowed to decay every year, whilst scarce a single mushroom of the common kind is allowed to remain for twenty-four hours wherever the foot of man or boy can find access. This species would yield good ketchup, but in very small quantities; if, however, a few are added with other mushrooms, it greatly improves the flavour of the ketchup.

The Rev. Gerard Smith thus describes the general character of the circles on the grass found where these mushrooms do grow, and which were long attributed to—

> "The nimble elves
> That do by moonshine green sour ringlets make,
> Whereof the ewe bites not; whose pastime 'tis
> To make these midnight mushrooms."

"Fairy-rings consist, generally speaking, of circles or parts of circles of grass, of a darker colour and more luxuriant growth than the surrounding herbage, the outer edge of the circle being well defined, while the colour and stature of the grass diminish and fade so gradually inwards, that it is difficult to determine the exact limit of the ring towards the centre. Very commonly there is to be observed an outer and contiguous ring, much narrower than the inner, and of which the grass is either short and weak, or faded and brown, remarkably contrasting with the vivid green of the inner ring : on this brown ring, or just upon its margin, fungi are found. The duration of fairy-rings varies much ; some disappear in a few weeks, others endure for years. A severe winter will obliterate the external traces of a ring, and prevent the usual crop of fungi appearing upon it at the proper season ; but such rings often reappear, and are thus considered to have been suddenly formed. During the whole course of their appearance the rings increase in-diameter, spreading outwards from the centre, the faded brown circle becoming rank with green and copious grass, and a fresh outer circle being formed of dead or feeble blades of grass. The rate of increase is various, some enlarging their diameter a few inches in the year, others as many feet. The circles frequently meet in the course of this gradual enlargement. In such cases the point of contact becomes obliterated ; and when this contact occurs between the margin of several such rings, the obliteration of the parts which meet leaves a variety of segments of circles upon the turf, which, pursuing an independent course, and some increasing more rapidly than others, present eventually an unaccountable irregularity, and, as it were, patchwork of greener and paler, stronger and weaker, portions of turf. When the turf is cut through such a ring at two contiguous

points, so that a breadth is taken up from the inner
rank green, through the faded breadth, to the outer
ordinary state, the soil of the faded ring is always found
drier and of a paler colour than the adjoining parts,
and abundantly impregnated with mycelium.   Indeed,
a careful examination will show that the faded and
impoverished condition of the turf of the outer ring is
due to the close investment of its roots by the mycelium
of the fungi which occupy the ring.   The dimensions
of the rings vary from three feet to three hundred feet
in diameter ; they are at times very irregular in form,
an accident arising either from the nature of the soil
and the obstacles which they meet with in their circum-
ferential expansion, or from more than one ring
coalescing, and producing an outline of undulating
curves."

That these fairy-rings were the nightly haunts and
dancing-grounds of fairy-folk was a general belief
before the existence of these little people came to be
doubted.   One old author writes, " They had always
fine music among themselves, and danced in a moon-
shiny night, around, or in a ring, as one may see at
this day upon every common in England where mushrooms grow."   Numerous conjectures were ventured
as to the origin of these rings when their fairy history was no longer believed in.   They were attributed
to the exhalations of a fertile subterranean vapour,
to the burrowing of moles, to the effects of lightning,
and in 1807 Dr. Wollaston ascribed them to the
growth of certain species of Agarics, which so entirely

absorbed all nutriment from the soil beneath that the herbage was for a while destroyed.

The Rev. M. J. Berkeley, an excellent authority, writes of them: " These rings are sometimes of very ancient date, and attain enormous dimensions, so as to be distinctly visible on a hill-side from a considerable distance. It is believed that they originate from a single fungus, whose growth renders the soil immediately beneath unfit for its reproduction. The spawn, however, spreads all around, and in the second year produces a crop whose spawn spreads again, the soil behind forbidding its return in that direction. Thus the circle is continually increased, and extends indefinitely till some cause intervenes to destroy it. If the spawn did not spread on all sides at first, an arc of a circle only is produced. The manure arising from the dead fungi of the former years makes the grass peculiarly vigorous round, so as to render the circle visible even when there is no external appearance of the fungus, and the contrast is often the stronger from that behind being killed by the old spawn. This mode of growth is far more common than is supposed, and may be observed constantly in our woods, · where the spawn can spread only in the soil or amongst the leaves and decaying fragments which cover it."*

One of the fairy legends associated with mushrooms is that of the two serving-girls at Tavistock, to whom the fairies were very kind. One of them by her neg-

---

* "Outlines of British Fungology," p. 41.

ligence having offended the little people, they proceeded
to her room and debated together as to what punish-
ment they should inflict.   This conversation the
unoffending one overheard, and it was to the effect
that her companion should have a lame leg for seven
years, and be ultimately cured by a herb growing
on Dartmoor, but with a name so long that the girl
could not remember it.   In the morning the other
girl arose lame, and continued so to the end of the period
assigned ; when, one day, as she was picking a mushroom, up started a strange-looking little boy, who
insisted upon striking her leg with a plant which he held
in his hand.   This was the magical plant, with which he
continued striking her leg till she became perfectly
cured, and one of the best dancers in the country.

Marasmius oreades is not the only fungus which has
this habit of growing in rings.   One of our largest gill-
bearing fungi, as well as some others, indulge in this
eccentricity,—probably, in times past to the great alarm
of the superstitious.

Marasmius scorodonius is largely consumed in
Austria, Germany, and some other continental countries.
It is known under the name of *Lauchschwamm* and
Hagyma gomba ; but neither these nor its garlic odour
would commend it to our own countrymen.   This little
species grows in dry pastures and on heaths.   It has a
tough and crisped reddish pileus, a hollow smooth reddish-brown stem, and dirty-white gills.   Although plentiful in the countries already named, it is rare with us.

Two or three other species might also be enumerated,

Boletus edulis

T. Way. 3 Wellington S? Strand Imp

equal, if not superior, to the latter for culinary purposes; but their inconstant or limited occurrence would only serve to raise expectations not likely to be realized.

Five other genera complete the order *Agaricini*, all more or less tough and dry, becoming at length hard and corky. In *Lentinus* the sharp edges of the tough gills are toothed, and in *Panus* they are equally sharp and tough, but not toothed. In *Xerotus* the tough gills are forked, but with blunt or obtuse edges; and the two divisions into which the gills separate are spreading or rolled back in *Schizophyllum*. In *Lenzites* the whole substance is corky, and the gills are often so connected by lateral branches as to form irregular cavities resembling pores.

PORE-BEARING FUNGI.

THE observing eye of the lover of nature in all its Protean forms will have discovered fungi, which in external contour resembled those we have already described, being furnished with a cap or pileus supported upon a stem ; but when more closely examined have been found to present the important distinction of having the under surface of the pileus not divided into plates or gills, but apparently perforated with small holes, as if pricked with a pin by some fairy in childish sport. Others, again, entirely devoid of a stem, and in some instances of extraordinary size and as tough as leather, or hard and unyielding as cork or wood, with the under or sometimes upper surface similarly perforated.

And, again, yet others of a waxy, or almost gelatinous texture, with wrinkles or folds more or less imperforated ; all of which are botanically united into a group, or natural order, in which the pores distinguish them from the gill-bearing order, and to which the distinctive appellation of *Polyporei* has been given. It requires no great erudition to arrive at the conclusion that this name has been given in allusion to the numerous pores with which one or other of the surfaces of these fungi are studded, derived from the Greek word *polus*, signifying *many*. These pores are the extremities of more or less connected tubes, upon the walls or inner linings of which the hymenium, or fructifying surface, supporting the reproductive bodies, or spores, is borne. Like the *Agaricini*, this order is again subdivided into smaller groups, or genera, in each of which the individuals agreeing most intimately with each other are associated. In the first genus, *Boletus* (*bolos*, Greek, a ball), the tubes are separable from one another. In *Polyporus* the pores are not easily, if at all, separable. In *Dœdalea* the pileus is corky and hard, and the pores are labyrinthiform, irregular, or torn. The remaining genera are briefly characterized in the Tabular arrangement of Orders and Genera with which this work concludes.

Upwards of thirty species of *Boletus* are British, and one of the commonest of these (*B. edulis*) in the opinion of some is scarcely inferior to the best mushroom in flavour. It has a smooth, brownish pileus, with tubes at first yellowish but becoming greenish or

green as it advances in age. For esculent purposes
they should be collected whilst still yellow. The stem
is reticulated, especially towards the summit, with a
delicate, pinkish network of fine lines (Pl. 15). It is
frequent in woods, especially in the South of England,
and is well diffused and appreciated on the continent of
Europe. Frequently it will attain a large size, so that
two or three of them are sufficient to furnish a family
with a meal. The best feature by which to distinguish
this species from its congeners is the reticulation of the
stem. It would be well to notice if the flesh changes
colour when bruised or cut, for the juice of the most
unwholesome species of this genus speedily turns blue
on exposure to the air. Dr. Badham says that "the
best manner of cooking this fungus must be left to be
decided by the taste of the gourmand; in every way
it is good. Its tender and juicy flesh, its delicate and
sapid flavour, render it equally acceptable to the plain
and to the accomplished cook. It imparts a relish
alike to the homely hash and the dainty ragout, and
may be truly said to improve every dish of which it is
a constituent." Mr. Berkeley takes exception to its
excellence, and gives as the result of his experience
that it is very moderate eating. Our own knowledge,
and that of gentlemen of our acquaintance who are
much greater amateurs of fungi, hold rather to the
opinion of Dr. Badham; but tastes are universally
allowed to vary. The ancient Romans are believed to
have employed this species of *Boletus*, and, apart from
their predilection for snails, cossi, and other delicacies

which we do not nowadays admire, were, on the whole, not bad judges of dainties.

In Lorraine this species is eaten under the name of Polish Mushroom, because, it is said, certain Poles first showed by their own example that these *Boleti* could be eaten without danger. In Russia they are strung on threads and dried for future use. When the fasts of the Greek Church come round, these dried fungi are in requisition, being prepared by simple simmering in water till they become soft. In the department of Gironde, in France, great quantities are preserved in this manner and sent annually to the Parisian markets, and when required for use are soaked in lukewarm water, or beef gravy, till they become softened, and are then cooked in the same manner as when in the fresh state. French cookery has devised many variations in the art of preparing this, as well as almost every other commonly used fungus, for the gastronome. There is certainly a kind of sliminess about the *Boleti* which would not commend them to the tastes of many ; but this becomes far more unpleasantly evident in some methods of preparation than others. They are, nevertheless, in any way better than no dinner at all, and if our rural population could be induced to look upon them with a little more favour, they would often get a relish with their " potatoes and point " for the trouble of collecting and cooking, while the *Boleti* are now permitted to flourish and decay year by year without care or regret.

In all cases the young state, while the under surface

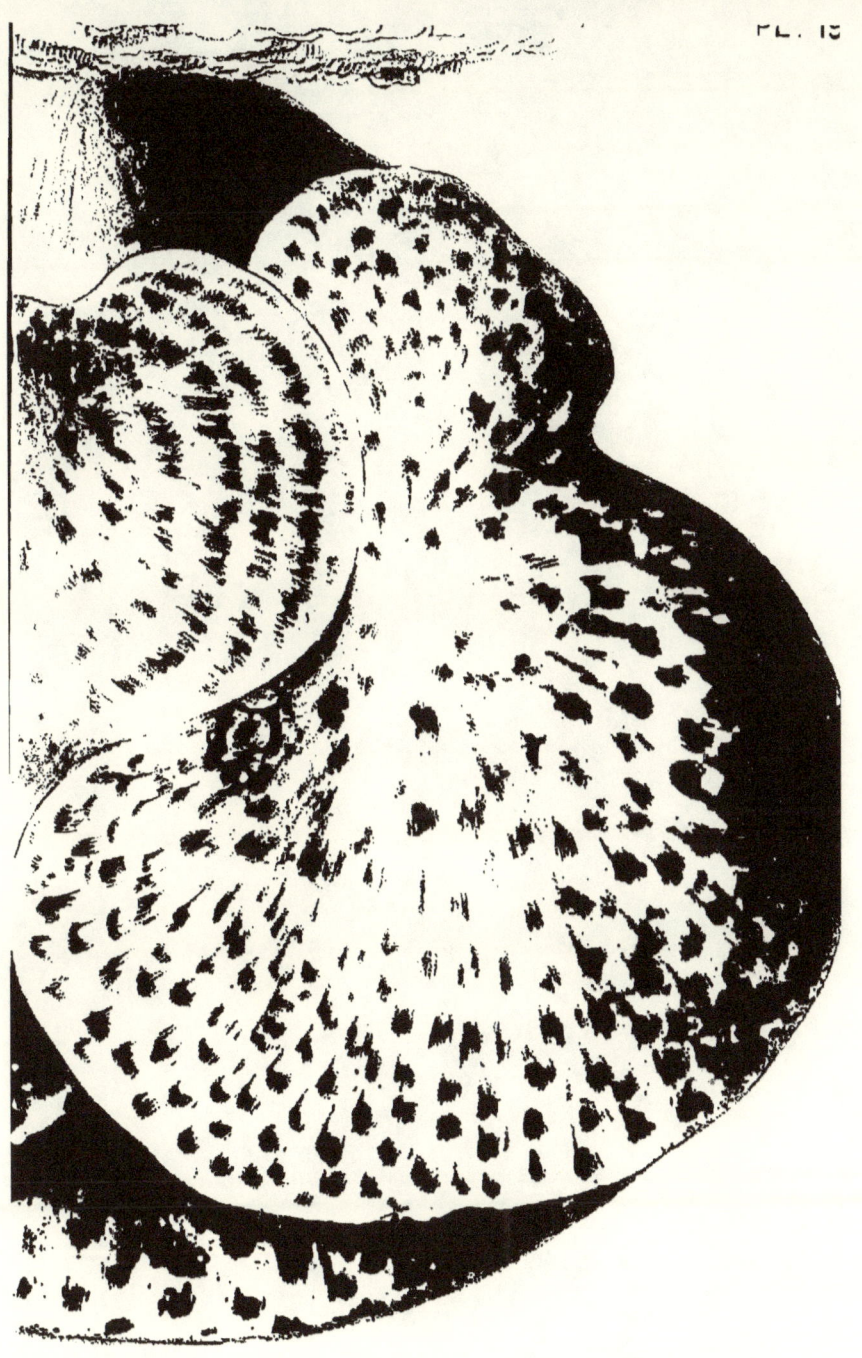

is still of a pale yellow, is preferable. One ready method of preparation consists in removing the stem, clearing away the pores, and then drawing off all super-fluous moisture upon a gridiron, wiping them, and after-wards stewing them with olive oil, parsley, garlic, pepper and salt, adding, when nearly ready, a little lemon-juice. In the rural districts of France they are simply cooked on the gridiron, and seasoned with salt and pepper, or fried in a pan with butter or oil. M. Roques states, that in the Lower Pyrenees the farm servants and others regale themselves with these fungi, baked on a dish and seasoned with oil, garlic, and parsley. This sometimes forms their principal meal.

For a stew, or soup, half a dozen young Boleti are put into a stewpan, with salt, pepper, a little grated nutmeg, a pound of lean ham minced small, half a pound of bread-crumbs, and a quarter of a pound of fresh butter. These are then placed over a brisk fire for an hour, care being taken to add from time to time a little beef gravy. The stew is then strained, and put on the fire again to simmer for twenty minutes, adding beef gravy according to taste. It is finally poured into a soup-tureen upon crusts of bread cut in pieces.

A gregarious species (*B. bovinus*) may be found growing in heathy localities, and especially in fir woods. The pileus is reddish grey, sometimes tinged with purple, and the angular tubes are of a greyish yellow, ultimately becoming of a rusty brown. The spores in this species are yellowish. The taste and smell is sweetish and agreeable; and Krombholz says it is much sought after abroad as a dish, and is good when dried.

Another species of Boletus (*B. scaber*) is very common in woods, but, though esculent, does not enjoy so good a reputation as the last. The tubes are white or dingy, the stem rather rough, and it is much inferior in respect of size, smell, and flavour to *Boletus edulis.*

Boletus castaneus, a small species with a velvety, cinnamon-coloured pileus and stem, short, white, and afterwards yellowish tubes, and white unchanging flesh, is rarely found in woods, and, although eaten on the Continent, is of inferior flavour.

An elegant Boletus (*B. elegans*) is found in woods, especially of firs, which is remarkable for the brilliant golden-yellow tint, and its pileus being viscid in moist weather; the flesh is of a pale yellow, and though said to be eatable, is certainly not worthy of recommendation.

Two other species (*B. impolitus* and *B. æstivalis*), also found in woods or woodland pastures, have the reputation of being wholesome, but are not of sufficient importance or value to make a description of them necessary.

It will be advisable to caution all who are inexperienced in collecting *Boleti* for alimentary purposes, and who may yet desire to make trial of them, that numerous species of *Boletus* are common to Great Britain, and several of these are unwholesome, some decidedly poisonous. If, upon cutting or bruising any specimen, it should be found to change colour, it should

be rejected. Some species become blue almost immediately upon wounding. Those with reddish stems, or
with the edges of the tubes, *i. e.* the under surface of
the pileus, red or crimson, should also be rejected.

The large *B. satanas,* the very name of which
conveys. suspicion, should be guarded against. It is
occasionally found in woods. The under surface of the
pileus appears of a blood-red colour, as also the stem.

The spores of the *Boleti* may be collected for examination in the same manner as already described for the
Agarics. In many instances they will be found to be
coloured, and in some of a beautiful roseate tint. The
prevailing colour will be some shade of palish or reddish
brown, white being the exception rather than the rule.

The genus *Polyporus* has the pores not easily separable, they being closely packed and united together.
The substance of the hymenophorum descends between
the pores, where it is called the trama. This is not the
case in *Boletus ;* for in that genus the hymenophorum
is quite distinct from the pores.

This genus is a very large one, and contains every
intermediate texture of substance from succulence or
pulpiness to the hardness and density of wood. We
remember a slice from one of the latter species being
sent to us for identification, with a number of specimens
of wood, and which was supposed to be "some kind of
palm wood." Forms are as varied as texture, and colour
as devious as form. Some have stems which are central,
others that are lateral, but the majority are without
stems at all.

A very familiar species (*P. squamosus*) of those having a lateral stem is found on almost every decayed ash, and sometimes on other trees.   It has a pale ochre-tinted pileus, somewhat of a fan shape, with the surface covered with darker scales (Pl. 19).   The stem is thick and dark-coloured, the pores running some distance down it.   It is extremely various in size, occasionally attaining enormous dimensions, perhaps seven feet in circumference, and weighing forty-two pounds. We have already alluded to the rapidity of its growth.*   We have seen drawings of exceedingly curious forms that have been found growing in cellars. , The edible qualities of this species cannot be declared first-rate. Mrs. Hussey, who is a very good judge in such matters, says one might as well think of eating saddle-flaps. Young specimens, before they have acquired the leathery consistency, would serve for an occasional meal.   In this stage they are prepared for the table in some parts of the Continent. A more suitable application, and one strongly recommended to those who, in these hirsute days, require such an instrument, is to select a large tough specimen, and after drying it carefully, cut it into shape, and employ it as a razor strop. A person who has had one in use for many years, says that it is far superior to the majority of those offered for sale. Another Polyporus (*P. betulinus*), without a stem, and not uncommonly found growing on birch-trees, is equally available for the same purpose.

Two other species are recommended as esculent,

* Page 6.

although neither of them is at all common in our islands; they are both of them peculiar in appearance, from being broken up into numerous pilei, so as to look like a dense cluster of separate individuals.

P. intybaceus, the first of these, is strongly recommended, and sometimes attains so large a size that one fungus will weigh forty pounds and suffice for the meal of a very large family. In cooking this species, it is advisable to cut off the darker coloured pileus, and only employ the white branching stem : when prepared in this way, it is equal to any Agaric we possess, according to the testimony of some, whilst all agree that it is excellent. The odour is inviting, and we would advise any who may meet with it to condemn it to the stew-pan.

P. giganteus is the other species to which we have alluded, and which, with *P. intybaceus*, is more common on the Continent, where its esculent qualities are known and duly appreciated. Both of these are found growing on the trunks of trees, and sometimes attain extraordinary dimensions.

The trunks of trees, of various kinds, are often found bearing a very conspicuous sulphur-coloured fungus (*P. sulfureus*), consisting of a number of overlapping pilei of the consistence of a mellow cheese. When wounded, it exudes copiously a yellow juice, which has been employed in dyeing, though it is doubtful whether it is of any great value for such a purpose. As this fungus dries, it becomes covered with beautiful crystals of oxalate of potash, which might suggest the presence of more active properties than the majority of the members of this genus possess. During decomposition this plant emits a bright phosphorescent light, a feature not common in our native fungi, and which makes this an object of curiosity, although we need scarcely add that it is entirely unfit for food.

The dry-rot of oak-built vessels is a species belonging to this genus (*P. hybridus*), whilst the common dry-rot of fir timber is a species of *Merulius*.

A curious leathery substance, known under the name of *Amadou*, or *German tinder*, found in tobacconists' shops, occasionally in sheets, or irregularly-shaped pieces, but more commonly manufactured into *fusees*, gives but little external evidence of its fungoid origin. This substance is obtained from several species of *Polyporus*, and consists of slices of these hard and corky Fungi, beaten out till they have become quite soft and flexible, then saturated in a solution of saltpetre and dried. At one time it was rather extensively employed in medical practice as a styptic, but is now seldom resorted to in England. On the Continent it is still an article of commerce, and in Northern Europe the smoker would almost as soon think of venturing abroad without his tobacco and pipe as without a supply of Amadou to rekindle his extinguished fire. One of the species usually employed in the manufacture of this article is *P. fomentarius*, a stemless species common on the trunks of trees.

Trametes and *Dædalea* are genera containing no species of economic value. The latter includes a fungus which, from its corky, rugged nature and common occurrence, is likely to interest the young mycologist. *Dædalea quercina* grows on oak-stumps, sometimes to a large size, spreading out from its support in a semicircular manner, and having the under surface broken up into a number of long, irregular, wavy fissures, as 'if the walls of several contiguous tubes had been broken down. Another equally common species (*D. unicolor*), with a zoned or banded pileus, may be met with on stumps. The peculiar form of the pores is one of the chief features of the genus.

In *Merulius*, the genus which succeeds it, the texture is not of the woody character of *Dædalea*, but on the contrary soft and waxy, and the hymenium is disposed in porous or wavy-toothed folds. The only popularly known species is one which unfortunately is too well known under the name of dry-rot. This name must not be supposed to indicate that the fungus is itself dry, or is caused by the absence of moisture,— the contrary of this being the case; but probably on account of its ravages reducing the structure upon which it establishes itself to a kind of dust. The *Merulius lacrymans* (*lacrymo*, Lat., I weep) is often dripping with moisture, as if weeping in regret for the havoc it has made. It is found sometimes attaining a dimension of several feet, and to check or prevent its ravages numerous experiments have been instituted, none having resulted in the discovery of a remedy thoroughly effective, though saturation with creosote appears to be the best.

G

The last genus in this order is *Fistulina*, which bears much external and general resemblance to *Polyporus*, and was at one time included in it; but is now separated on account of the hymenium being at first covered with little pap-like elevations which afterwards elongate into distinct tubes bearing the reproductive bodies. The only species we possess is termed *F. hepatica* (*hepar*, Lat., the liver), from its colour, which resembles that of liver. This fungus assumes a great variety of forms. In its earliest stages it sometimes looks like a strawberry, when more advanced it has often the appearance of a tongue. One of its continental local names is *Lingua di Castagna*, which applies to this resemblance. It is a fleshy, juicy fungus, with an undivided, unstalked pileus, and when cut presents a bright streaky appearance, not unlike beetroot, and contains a red juice; the porous under-surface is yellowish or flesh-coloured (Pl. 18) The trunks of old oaks are very commonly the habitat of this species, which occasionally attains a very large size. When old, it becomes rather tough, but in all its stages it affords an excellent gravy, and, when young, if sliced and grilled, would pass for a good beefsteak. Specimens are now and then met with that would furnish four or five men with a good dinner; and they have been collected weighing as much as thirty pounds. The liver-colour and streaky interior are sufficient guides whereby to recognize this species under all its protean forms. Mrs. Hussey says of it, that "if it is not beef itself, it is sauce for it;" and she recommends that it should be

sliced and macerated with salt after the manner of
making mushroom ketchup. The deep red liquor that
is produced should be put hot into a dish with a little
lemon-juice and minced shalots, and a broiled rump-
steak deposited in it. Great will be the surprise of the
epicure at the quantity of gravy the steak has afforded,
greater still when told that it is the simple juice of
a fungus; for the similitude to the juice of beef is
exact. The ketchup must be strained from the substance raw, and afterwards boiled with spice for keeping
like ordinary ketchup. It should not be employed but
to represent beef gravy, as it does not possess the flavour
of mushrooms. In France, where this species is also
eaten, it is first washed and dried, then placed in boiling
water for a short time, and afterwards stewed with
butter, parsley, scallion, pepper and salt; yolk of egg
being afterwards added, when the stew is ready for the
table. It is also grilled. In Vienna it is cut in thin
slices and eaten with salad as we employ beetroot, and
is also cooked with meat, adding a little cream or lemon-
juice. It will be found necessary, whichever method of
cooking is adopted, to employ fresh specimens, as they
will shrivel up and become leathery if sliced and dried.
The best mode of preserving for future use is by con-
verting them into the kind of sauce or gravy to which
we have alluded.

TEETH-BEARING FUNGI.

THE third order of fungi is termed *Hydnei*, from *Hydnum* (*udna*, Gr., puffs resembling mushrooms), the typical genus. In this order we encounter numerous spines, teeth, or pap-like projections from the surface, over which the hymenium is spread, and bearing the spores. The order is not a very large one, but is distinct in its features from the preceding.

In *Hydnum* the spines are awl-shaped, and distinct or separate at the base. This structure will be better understood by a reference to our plate (Pl. 16), in which a portion of the pileus of *Hydnum repandum* is shown in section magnified. This species is common on the ground in woods and woody places, and has a compact wavy pileus, with spines of unequal length proceeding from the under surface, which is rather paler in colour. There is a variety much redder than our plate, which has been treated as a distinct species under the name of *rufescens*, but which appears to be the same in every feature except colour. The flesh of this fungus is firm and white, rather hot to the taste when raw, but mild when cooked.

On account of its containing less than the average amount of water in its composition, it may be dried successfully, and in this state preserved for winter use. It is employed as food in Austria and Belgium, as well as in France, in all of which localities it is a common

1 Hydnum imbricatum
2 Hydnum repandum

.C. del.   E. Cooke

species. From the firmness of its texture it may be concluded that young and fresh specimens are the best, and the cooking operations should be carefully performed. The method recommended is to cut them in pieces, steep them in warm water, and afterwards stew them in a rich brown sauce. Roques says that after steeping they should be cooked in hog's lard with pepper, salt, parsley, and beef gravy, taking care that they are cooked long enough to become tender.

Singularly enough, this species has suffered under the imputation of being poisonous ; but this was evidently destitute of foundation, for M. Roques says that himself and friends scoured the woods of Malmaison, "where we gathered a dish of these champignons, which I prepared myself with butter, verjuice, grated nutmeg, pepper, salt, a point of garlic, and some spoonfuls of chicken broth. This ragout, poured over some thin toasted bread, well browned, was served at table, and was greatly relished by all the guests. In France this species is known locally by the name of *Eurchon, Rignoche,* and *Arresteron;* in the Vosges as *Barbe de vache* (cow's beard) and *Pied de mouton* (sheep's foot).

The scaly-capped Hydnum (*H. imbricatum*) is found but rarely in our pine woods; but when once seen is not likely to be forgotten. Our plate (Pl. 16) will give a very good idea of its general appearance, and experience the best test of its esculent properties, which are affirmed to be fully equal to those of any other member of the genus. It is much more common on the continent of

Europe than with us, where it is regarded equally with *H. repandum,* and in Austria especially it is included amongst the esculent species.

H. coralloides in its early stages greatly resembles a cauliflower; it is whitish and very much branched, differing in appearance from any fungus which hitherto we have encountered. It occurs on decayed trees and stumps, especially of fir, beech, and ash. This is said to be fully equal to *H. repandum,* but unfortunately it, as well as the succeeding species, is rare in our country.

H. caput-Medusæ has very much the same habit and appearance, being branched in a similar manner, but has ultimately a greyish tint. It is also found on the trunks of trees. Though rarely occurring in France, it is common in Italy and in parts of Austria, where it is reckoned among the edible species. The flavour of both these is said to resemble greatly that of the common mushroom.

No other species is recorded in this or the remaining seven genera of the order, as of any service to man. The student will find at the end of the volume the names and characters of these genera, with an indication of the number of indigenous species.

———

LEATHERY FUNGI.

THE fourth order, *Auricularini,* has distinct peculiarities; but as no member is of sufficient importance, on account of the absence of economic properties, to claim our notice, we will not attempt the somewhat difficult task of defining it so as to be comprehended by our non-scientific readers, except by stating in general terms that the hymenium or fructifying surface is almost destitute of folds or projections. No fungus is more common or better known than *Stereum hirsutum*, which is found on stumps everywhere. The leathery pileus spreading out from its matrix, hairy on its upper surface, of a colour bordering upon olive, zoned with a darker tint, and bearing a yellowish margin. In size it is generally three or four inches across, and several pilei are often closely arranged one above another. Many others in this group are nearly equally common, did the limits of our work permit of their description and illustration, but as more important genera are still unnoticed we must content ourselves with again referring to the synopsis.

CLUB-BEARING FUNGI.

IN this order (*Clavariei*) another change of form takes place. We have herein, grouped together, a series of club-shaped, or branched, fleshy fungi, with the hymenium scarcely distinct from the portion which bears it, and often obtaining a great expansion of surface by means of multiplied and intricate ramifications. The most beautiful examples are not met with in Britain, but those which we have may serve to give a general idea of the more magnificent kinds which vegetate in the Alpine regions of Europe. Some of the species have white and others yellowish spores. The former are nearly all wholesome, the latter seldom. It has, however, been distinctly affirmed that none of them are dangerous. Small specimens of some of the edible kinds are represented in our plate in company with a species of *Geoglossum* (Pl. 17) ; the latter being added for comparison, belonging as it does to a different order, to which a brief reference will be made, and which does not furnish any kinds that are esculent. ·

Clavaria rugosa is not an uncommon inhabitant of woods, but is generally so small, and sparingly distributed, as not to repay collecting for esculent purposes. This species may be found either simply club-shaped, delicately white, and with longitudinal furrows, or with the tip more or less lobed, or with decided branches proceeding from the axis. Occasionally it is found of a dirty white, or with a bluish-grey tinge. If laid upon a piece of slate or black paper, the white spores will be thrown down. All the white-spored Clavarias are wholesome, but some are so tough and leathery, and others so small, that the number at all available for alimentary purposes is limited. They should, after being collected, be washed in luke-warm water and perfectly dried, then tied together in little bundles like asparagus, and cooked with butter, parsley, onion, pepper, and salt ; when cooked, they may be improved by the addition of a little cream and the yolk of an egg. It has also been recommended that a few spoonfuls of stock be added during the cooking.

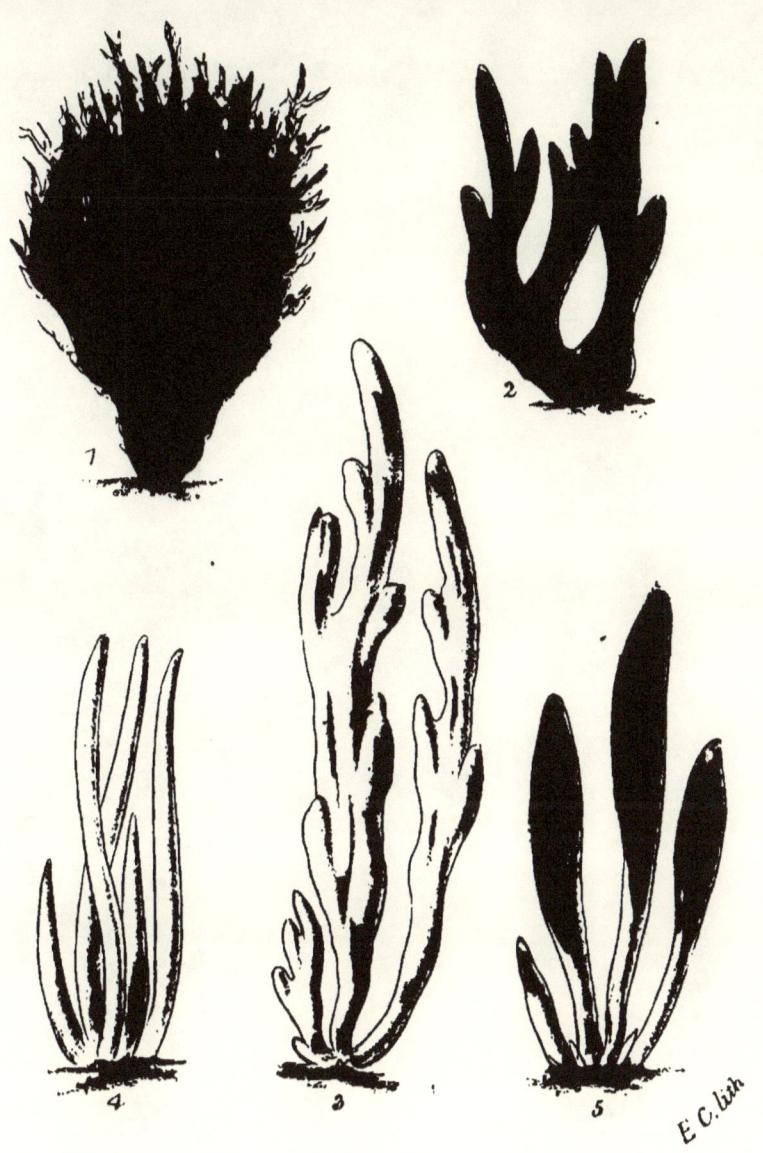

E.C.lith

1 Clavaria cinerea   2.C amethystina   3. C rugosa
4.C vermiculata 5.Geoglossum olivaceum

Roques states that at Vienna they are fricasseed with butter and sweet basil.

A fleshy, much-branched species, with red tips (*C. Botrytis*), is rare in this country, but is common in the Vosges, and in Carinthia, where it is usually eaten.

The cinereous Clavaria (*C. cinerea*) is common in woods in some districts. It has a short thick stem, is very much branched and irregular, and becomes ultimately of a cinereous hue. The substance is brittle, and not tough as in some species. In France this is known under various names, as *Pied de coq*, *Gallinole*, &c., and in Italy as *Ditola rossa*, in both which countries it is eaten.

An extremely common clustered yellow species is found in pastures (*C. fastigiata*), and although some authors have proscribed all the yellow species, Roques affirms that it is equally good eating with those generally esteemed as the best, and that in Germany it is eaten under the name of *Ziegenbart* (goat's beard).

The most beautifully coloured species (*C. amethystina*) found in Britain is rare and small, so that it would be vain to seek sufficient to constitute a dish. It is not plentiful on the Continent, where it is preferred by some to all the other species, and is said to possess a very fine flavour.

The coral-like Clavaria (*C. coralloides*) has rather a thick stem, is much and irregularly branched, white, hollow, with a mushroomy odour and agreeable taste. It is an inhabitant of woods, but not a plentiful species on this side the Channel. It is found commonly and much esteemed in Germany, Italy, Switzerland, &c. In these countries they are preserved for winter use by being plunged in boiling water, dried, and macerated in vinegar.

Probably others of our indigenous kinds are edible, especially one resembling *C. fastigiata*, which is found on lawns, and is of a tint of palish umber, not at all inclining to yellow; and *C. cristata*, which, as well as *C. rugosa*, is found in woods.· Should either of these be found in sufficient quantity they certainly merit the trouble of an experiment.

The three remaining genera of this order contain no species calling for notice.

GELATINOUS FUNGI.

THE last order of the first family of Fungi is *Tremellini*, in which the whole plant is gelatinous, and more or less folded. The fructifying surface is always uppermost, spread over, and following all its foldings and inequalities. With but one exception, this order is unhonoured in history or romance, and unknown as food or physic. The exception is in favour of the Jew's ear (*Hirneola auricula-Judæ*), which had at one time a reputation for the cure of sore throats, and also as a topical astringent, and even now it has some repute abroad, or it would not appear amongst the medicinal substances sent to the International Exhibition from one of the French colonies. Its faculty of absorbing and holding water like a sponge has resulted in its use as a medium for applying eye-water to weak or diseased eyes, and similar purposes. Of late years it is seldom to be met with in the herbalists' shops, and, in England at least, its reputation and "occupation's gone." The curious name it has appropriated to itself may be traced to the ear-like form which it sometimes assumes. It is not uncommonly found on elder stumps, and sometimes on elms. A variety, shaped something like a bird's nest, has obtained the distinctive appellation of *Nidularia*, but its forms are by no means permanent.

The six orders already described, and in part illustrated, constitute that most important group called *Hymenomycetes*, from the fact of the hymenium being the most prominent feature. Space will not permit of our entering so fully into the particulars of the succeeding groups, which need be less regretted as many of the members are exceedingly minute, and scarce any present features of equal interest with those which have hitherto occupied our attention.

PERIDIATE FUNGI.

THE second family of fungi is termed *Gasteromycetes* (*Gaster*, Gr., a stomach ; *mukes*, a mushroom), which, though in common with many others to be found in the Appendix, a long and complicated name, truly represents the features of the group to which it is applied. Herein the hymenium, or spore-bearing surface, is inclosed within a covering called a peridium (from *perideo*,

Gr., I wrap round), so that all the spores are produced and ripened within a kind of stomach or *gaster*; and from this feature the family bears the name of *Gasteromycetes*. Every one knows the puff-ball, a spherical pouch, containing, when ripe, an almost impalpable brownish dust, not unlike Scotch snuff, and which mischievous schoolboys delight in puffing in each other's faces. The pouch is the peridium or stomach, and the brown dust the innumerable ripened spores. But puff-balls are not the sole members of this group; they constitute but one of five orders.

SUBTERRANEAN FUNGI.

CERTAIN fungi having such a structure as we have described, are subterranean in habit, and these are included in the first order under the name of *Hypogæi* (*upo*, Gr., under; *gea*, the earth). In these fungi the hymenium does not become dusty, but remains permanent; nor does it melt away as in other groups, except when it becomes decayed. Some of these resemble truffles so nearly as to be confounded with them. One species of *Melanogaster* is sold in the markets of Bath under the name of red truffle, and is therefore edible. This is the only example which has come to our knowledge of a useful species. *Melanogaster variegatus* is found under trees, especially in the neighbourhood of beeches, in the south and south-western counties of England, and resembles, externally, a brownish irregular tuber; internally it is divided into cells by whitish

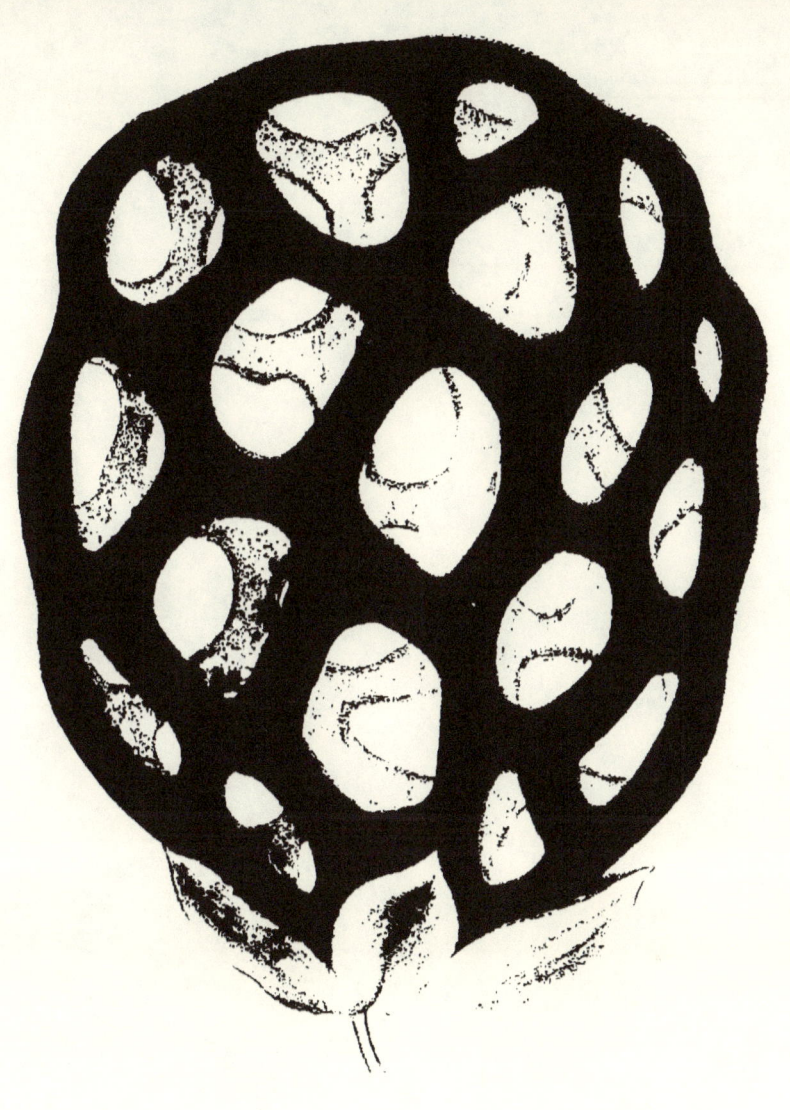

Clathrus cancellatus

M. Cooke lith.

walls, containing at first a black pulp, and ultimately a number of minute dark spores (Pl. 23, fig. 2). The surface of the red truffle is smooth and not covered with warts or tubercles as in the true truffle. It is believed that the taste and aroma of this species is inferior to that of the truffle, although it may be employed as a substitute when the genuine article is scarce. Although we have employed the term *subterranean* as representative of *Hypogæi*, and applied it to this order, it must not, therefore, be concluded that it includes all fungi which are subterranean in habit, as the Truffles, for instance, are excluded, and must be sought for in the Sporidiiferous families.

STINKHORN FUNGI.

An acquaintance with the members of this order, which is known botanically as *Phalloidei*, will convince any one of the propriety of assigning to them not only their common English but also their scientific Grecian name. Some of them are rare, but the common stinkhorn will serve as a type, and answer as a convincing argument in both cases.

One of the most striking in appearance, disgusting in odour, and noxious in properties of all fungi, is the Latticed Stinkhorn (*Clathrus cancellatus*), which is, however, so rare as scarcely to merit a notice here except to call attention to its only commendable feature, that of the beauty and singularity of its form (Pl. 20). The receptacle resembles a spherical network or latticework of coral, but is of so putrescent a nature that its odour materially detracts from its beauty; and it is recorded of a botanist who gathered one for the purpose of drying it for his herbarium, that he was compelled by the stench to rise during the night and cast the offender out at the window. M. Roques relates of its properties that a young person having eaten a morsel was seized with violent convulsions, lost the use of her speech, and ultimately fell into a stupor which lasted forty-eight hours: prompt attention was given to her, but it appears to have been some months before she was perfectly cured.

The common Stinkhorn (*Phallus impudicus*) has an equally abominable odour, to which we have already alluded,* with nothing of beauty to recommend it, and although not uncommon, no one would think of preparing it for a meal.

————

PUFF-BALL FUNGI.

In the first of the two orders just noticed the hymenium neither melts nor becomes dusty; in the last it melts, and in the present order it dries into a dusty mass of threads and spores. From the remote resemblance which this mass sometimes bears to a lock of soft brown wool, the order has been called *Tricho-gastres* (*Thrix*, Gr., wool or hair). The most picturesque of forms are found in the genus *Geaster;* but although we have nine indigenous species, none of these

* *Vide* p. 10.

are common. In these the peridium or covering is double, the outer one, bursting and dividing into separate lobes, falls back in a stellate manner at the base of the ball formed by the inner peridium, which latter ultimately opens and discharges its spores from the summit. Although useless, these are very curious and interesting fungi, and are not possessed of the strong and unpleasant odour of the members of the last group.

The genera *Bovista* and *Lycoperdon*, which follow, may be distinguished from each other by the bark of the former at length shelling off, and of the latter remaining attached in the form of scales or warts. There are but two species of *Bovista* indigenous to Britain, distinguished by the colour of the peridium, which in either instance supplies the specific name. *B. nigrescens* is blackish, and *B. plumbea* of a lead-colour. Although we have never heard of the former being eaten, it is stated that the latter furnishes a very palateable dish. *Bovista plumbea* and *Lycoperdon pyriforme* have, however, been so confounded together, sometimes in the name and sometimes in the individuals themselves, as evidenced by the fact that figures of the latter have been given with the name of the former, that one seems disposed to doubt whether both have not been eaten the one for the other, and whether both may not be esculent, though perhaps not excellent. Both species of *Bovista* are very common in pastures, and resemble little round balls, which, when ripe, discharge their dust-like spores from openings in the top of the papery peridium.

There is scarcely a dweller or stroller into the country

that has not seen the giant puff-ball (*Lycoperdon gigan-teum*), sometimes attaining the size of a child's head, and in its earlier stages of a dirty whitish colour, becoming browner by age, in which latter condition, if broken, it emits a cloud of snuff-coloured impalpable dust. Very few persons are, however, aware that when in its young and pulpy condition this *Lycoperdon* is excellent eating, and, indeed, has but few competitors for the place of honour at the table. It is especially esteemed in Italy, and would be with us, not only on account of the impossi-bility of confounding it with other species, on which account the repast may be enjoyed without fear, but also for its own intrinsic value. Unfortunately this fungus deteriorates very speedily after gathering, and should be discarded if, when cut, any yellow marks or stains are visible, for then it is too old. When the cut surface of the puff-ball is white as snow, then cut it up into slices of half an inch in thickness and fry it in fresh butter, adding according to your taste a sprinkling of pounded sweet herbs, pepper, and salt. Mrs. Hussey recom-mends that each slice be dipped in the yolk of an egg and sprinkled with chopped sweet herbs and spice. Then, she says, "they are much lighter and more digestible than egg omelettes, and resemble brain fritters."

My friend R. Ward, Esq., of Salhouse Hall, who is, by the bye, a connoisseur in edible fungi, writes, "We have a delicious dish in this fungus, which is not uncommon in some seasons in these parts. Sliced and seasoned with butter and salt, and fried in a pan, no French omelette is half so good in richness and delicacy of flavour. I am too glad to seize upon them when I can get them ; of course, in the soft pulpy state." This is not the only testimony we have of their excellence. Another connoisseur says, " The puff-ball makes such an excellent omelette, and is so much better than any mushroom I ever before tasted, that it ought not to be called mushroom." To this we may add our own experience, derived while this work is passing through the press. A gardener brought us a large puff-ball, equal in size to a half-quartern loaf, and which was still in its young and pulpy state, of a beautiful creamy whiteness when cut. It had been found developing itself in a garden at Highgate, and to the finder its virtues were unknown. We had this specimen cut in slices of about half an inch in thickness, the outer skin peeled off, and each slice dipped in an egg which had been beaten up, then sprinkled with bread-crumbs, and fried in butter, with salt and pepper. The result was exceedingly satisfactory ; and finding this immense fungus more than our family could consume whilst it remained fresh, we invited our friends to partake, and they were as delighted as ourselves with the new breakfast relish, to them, and to us—the first, but we hope not the last, experiment upon a fried puff-ball.

The great puff-ball has an ancient reputation for the stanching of blood, and was consequently dried and preserved by many a good housewife in days gone by, and is still considered by some of the antique dames of the past generations as a sovereign remedy for a cut finger.   The use of the spongy portion as a tinder must also be reckoned amongst the achievements of the past.   When burnt, the fumes of this fungus are said to possess a stupefying narcotic property ; in this form the Lycoperdon is still occasionally employed to stupefy bees, so that their hives may be robbed of the honey without danger.   Lately these fumes have been proposed and recommended as an anæsthetic in the place of chloroform.   But the most important of all uses is that of food, to which we have already alluded.

Lycoperdon cælatum is another common species scarcely attaining so large a size, and occasionally found growing in rings.   The spores in this species are yellowish, whilst in the great puff-ball they are of an olive-colour.   When this puff-ball is dried, it may be employed as amadon, first soaking it in a solution of nitre, and afterwards drying it.   It is questionable whether in any stage it is wholesome as food.

The pear-shaped puff-ball (*L. pyriforme*), to which allusion has already been made, may be found in clusters on almost any old decayed stump.   It is small and pear-shaped, as its name implies.   If good for food at all, it must be during its young state.

The remaining genera, *Scleroderma, Polysaccum,* and *Cenococcum,* contain no species of general interest. It has been stated that the powder from some of the *Sclerodermæ* is irritating to the eyes and nose, and that, taken inwardly, they are poisonous ; but for neither of these statements are we prepared to vouch.

The order next in rotation is *Myxogastres*, in which the entire mass is at first pulpy and gelatinous, becoming ultimately dusty. This is a remarkable group, sometimes presenting individuals exceedingly beautiful both in form and colouring; and were they not of such microscopic dimensions, they would certainly become popular favourites, only surpassed by some species of *Æcidium*, which would compete with them for the preference. Unfortunately, however, these beautiful creations are unknown, save to the privileged few who have, by the aid of the microscope, become acquainted, not only with these, but other minute denizens of a new floral world. As it constitutes a portion of the plan upon which this work was designed, that it should not include more than incidental references to species unappreciable by the naked eye, these and many succeeding groups, of greater or less extent, will have to be thus summarily dismissed.

It is probable that the young student of nature has found, and marvelled at, certain curious cup or crucible-shaped receptacles containing a number of roundish or elliptical bodies, which caused the whole to assume the appearance of a miniature birdsnest containing eggs, and hence procured for them the name of Birdsnest Fungi. These singular, but not uncommon productions, are members of the order *Nidulariacei* (*nidulus*, Lat., a little nest), so termed from the features alluded to. In this order the spores are compacted together into lenticular or similarly shaped masses, inclosed in a peridium, and several of these are contained within

an outer peridium, either open or closed ; this outer
peridium constituting the nest, and the compacted
masses of spores the eggs. This little order has not
more than four representatives in Britain.

DUST-LIKE FUNGI.

THE third group, or family, termed *Coniomycetes*,
consists of dust-like fungi in which the prominent
feature is the spores. The mycelium is often obsolete
and the threads short ; they are in some instances
naked, and in others inclosed. The spores are large in
proportion to the rest of the plant, and extremely abundant. We shall not attempt to characterize the different
divisions of this group, containing, as it does, objects so
minute and uninteresting to the general observer. There
are, however, some few facts which, even in a work of
this description, deserve to be recorded.

One section of this family includes the numerous
species of rust and mildew which are found all over the
world as parasites upon flowering plants. It was
doubted at one time whether these were plants at all,
and now that they are acknowledged as members of the
vegetable kingdom, are very much despised and neglected.
They may not present such beauties of form and colour
as to enchant the fashionable collector, or induce him to
stroll into the country in search of them ; but the agri-
culturist views them as amongst the pests of the farm, and,
if for no other reason, they deserve to be better known.

The *Pucciniæi* are developed on almost every

plant,—on wheat, grass, asparagus, mint, plum-leaves, beans, beet, oak, birch, poplar, sallow, willow, roses, violets, primroses, thistles, coltsfoot, &c. &c. The Dhoora corn of the tropics, and the maize of temperate regions, are not less certainly the victims of these parasites than the wheat, barley, and oats of our own land. It has been said, and we fear with some show of truth, that bunted wheat ground up into flour is largely used in the manufacture of gingerbread; in which case the colour is concealed on the one hand, and the taste on the other; and not having been found to be seriously injurious, no depreciation in gingerbread has resulted in consequence. Many species of *Æcidium* are exceedingly beautiful when viewed under the microscope. The clusters of brightly-coloured, urn-shaped bodies resemble the delicate waxy flowers of exotic heaths; but to the naked eye these appear only as rusty spots on the leaves or other portions of plants upon which they establish themselves.

In early spring the leaves of the pilewort (*Ranunculus ficaria*) will often be found with bright orange-coloured spots on the under surface and occasionally on the petioles. When viewed through a lens, these spots will be seen to consist of clusters of cup-shaped receptacles, fringed at the margin, and filled with minute, bright, dust-like spores. These are examples of *Æcidium ranunculacearum*, which is also found on other species of *Ranunculus*. There are species of *Æcidium* found flourishing on the living leaves of other plants equally interesting and beautiful.

THREADY FUNGI.

THE fourth group contains the *Hyphomycetes*, in which the threads are the principal feature. These threads, which bear the naked spores, are white, brown, or coloured, and the best known examples are those which bear the common name of *Moulds*. These are amongst the most insatiate of the fungoid race; scarce anything escapes them;—dead fungi or dead spiders, meal or sugar, cheese or onions, pears or oranges, linen or glass. Mouldy cheese may be relished, and pains taken to engraft or bud the plant upon others, yet the moulds are not always so harmless. In certain species they are decidedly poisonous. Turpin says that milk arrested for some time in the udder of a cow was found to contain mould, and species of fungi belonging to this group are not unfrequent in the lungs and stomach of the human subject in certain conditions of disease.

The yeast-plant is a fungus, or, to speak more precisely, a kind of *Penicillium*, growing and increasing almost indefinitely, and by a species of chemical action producing fermentation in any saccharine matter with which it is mixed. When microscopically examined, yeast will be found to consist of a multitude of ovoidal cells containing a nucleus. The fresh yeast consists of these individual cells; but after being mixed with the wort of

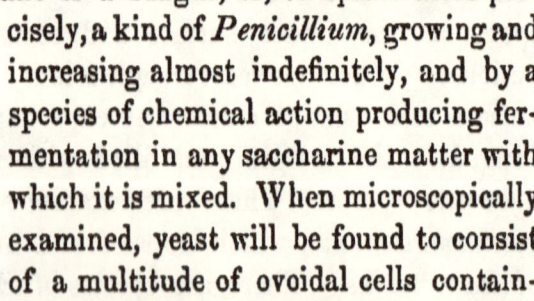

Fig. g.

beer for an hour, budding will have commenced (as in fig. *g*). These buds will ultimately increase to the size of the parent cells, and these will again bud; so that in six or eight hours a string of cells will be found to have been produced, attached to each other like a string of beads, with occasional lateral branches. Some authors have referred the yeast-plant to a low station in a subdivision of *Algæ*.

The vinegar-plant is of a similar nature, and both are more correctly included amongst those plants with which we have associated them. This view is supported by the most eminent mycologists of the present day.

MUCORACEOUS FUNGI.

THE fifth group or family, the *Physomycetes*, is a small one, at least so far as British examples are concerned, and forms an intermediate link between the *Sporiferous*, or naked-spored fungi, and the *Sporidiiferous*, or those in which the spores are inclosed, to which this group belongs. In the *Physomycetes*, the cells which contain the spores are bladder-shaped, and scattered upon threads, which are not compacted into a distinct hymenium. Like the true moulds, these minute plants are found upon decaying vegetable substances, especially articles of food. The bread-mould is a common and familiar example, and if, in this instance, decay has not already taken place, it is speedily accelerated.

SPORIDIIFEROUS FUNGI.

THE sixth and last group consists of the *Ascomycetes*,
in which the spores are developed in cells or bags, called
asci, often accompanied by abortive *asci* in the form of
threads, and termed paraphyses. These are produced
upon a cellular stratum, sometimes forming a cavity, or
envelope, which constitutes the *peridium*, and sometimes the *peridium* is absent. A portion of the members
of this group are subterranean in their habits ; and
though the majority of them are too small to serve as
articles of food, there are some which have great
repute amongst the lovers of delicious repasts.

In the order *Elvellacei* the hymenium becomes more
or less exposed. The substance is in most instances
fleshy, in others waxy, and the form is commonly either
cup-shaped or club-shaped. The genus *Peziza* contains some of the most elegant of British fungi, as in
the example (*Peziza aurantia*) given on our title-page,
and which was gathered amongst the grass on Hampstead Heath, early in November. It is by no means an
uncommon species, very beautiful, but of no economic
value. Another species (*P. coccinea*) is still more
beautiful both in form and colouring, but less common.
Almost every fallen twig of the larch will afford examples
of the little white and red *Peziza* (*P. elegans*). Two
other species, of more modest hue, have the recommendation of being esculent.

The sporidia of many of the *Pezizæ* are ejected from the hymenium with such force, and in such profusion, that they form a cloud or vapour of minute sporidia in the air around the plant from whence they are expelled. In some of the genera of this order the surface of the hymenium is greatly enlarged by folding or plaiting, so that there are deep fissures or cavities, which give such a distinct feature to the plants, that there is little fear of confounding them with other species.

In the order *Elvellacei* we meet externally and superficially with the appearance of a return to the pileated forms encountered in the commencement of our survey. The hymenium is at length more or less exposed, and sometimes borne on a stem. In the genus *Morchella* the hymenium is folded upon a stalked receptacle, these folds forming deep pits, at times irregular, at others definite in shape. In such species as have the pileus free at the base, the external contour reminds one at first of a conical-capped

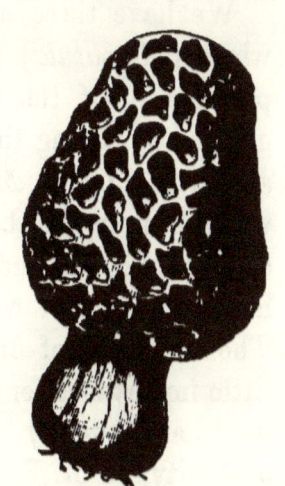

Fig. h.

Agaric; but this resemblance no longer obtains when it is remembered that the hymenium is borne on the upper surface, and not on the under, as in *Agarics* and *Boleti.*

The MORELL (*Morchella esculenta*) is chiefly employed in this country in the dried state as a seasoning

for soups, in which state they are imported. The
ordinary retail price is from one shilling to eighteen
pence an ounce. Although only employed here in its
dried state for seasoning, it is far more delicious when
fresh, and affords a liquor of much more exquisite
flavour than the ketchup of mushrooms. The demand
was formerly so great for morells in Germany, that the
peasantry were. induced to burn down the woodland in
immense tracts, on account of the more productive
nature of the burnt soil, until legislative enactments
put an end to the practice.

We have three native species of *Morchella*, one of
which (*M. patula*) is too rare to be of economic importance. Of the other two, *M. esculenta* is distinguished by having the base of the pileus attached to the
stem (fig. *h*). In *M. semilibera* the pileus is free half-
way up from its base. In the former the pileus is
commonly ovate, and in the latter conical. *M. esculenta*
is more a lover of woods, and *M. semilibera* of hedges.
The capability of distinguishing between the two is of
little importance for alimentary purposes, since both are
good, and equally esteemed abroad. We have the
authority of M. Roques for stating, that they are not
less esteemed in France than in Italy, in Germany than
in Switzerland, and in Brabant than in England. Some
give the preference to one kind, and some to the other ;
but both have nearly the same odour which gratifies the
smell, and the same flavour which pleases the taste ;
but they must not be gathered with the dew upon them.
Different methods of cooking morells are in vogue

in France. Amongst the most approved are the following :—

RAGOUT OF MORELLS.—Pick and clean your fungi and cut them in two, wash and dry them well by wiping, then put them in a stewpan with butter, place them over a brisk fire, and when the butter is melted, squeeze in a little lemon-juice, give a few turns, and then add salt, pepper, and a little grated nutmeg. Cook slowly for an hour, adding at intervals small quantities of beef gravy or jelly broth. When done, thicken with yolks of eggs.

Morells may also be treated in this fashion :—Put them upon the fire with butter, salt, pepper, and a small bundle of herbs. Simmer and add a little flour. Soften them with good beef gravy. Let them cook and reduce on a gentle fire, then remove the bundle of herbs. Fry some bread-crumbs in butter, then beat up the yolks of three eggs, add a pinch of powdered sugar, which mix with the morells, and pour the whole over the fried bread-crumbs, previously put into a dish.

MORELLS A LA ITALIENNE.—Pick, wash, and dry your morells. Cut them in two or three pieces according to size, and place them in a stewpan over a lively fire ; add olive oil, pepper, salt, and a bundle of herbs ; let them simmer some minutes, then add chopped parsley, a little onion, and a chive of garlic. Continue the cooking over a gentle fire. Soften with beef gravy and a glass of white wine. Serve with the piece of a lemon, and bread-crumbs fried brown and crisp.

Besides these ways, morells are eaten in a variety of styles ; but M. Roques affirms that there is none so delicate as a piece of veal surrounded with morells, suitably seasoned and cooked in an oven in its own juices.

In the genus *Helvella* the return to the forms of Hymenomycetal fungi seems to be still more complete, on account of the even manner in which the hymenium overspreads the surface, a feature distinguishing this genus from the preceding; but the student must not be led by the external appearance in opposition to important structural differences.

The best substitute for the expensive morell may be found in two indigenous species of *Helvella* (*H. crispa* and *H. lacunosa*). Like the morell, they may be collected during the season and dried, and thus preserved for use all the year round. He must be indeed an excellent judge and of a most exquisite taste, who can detect the difference in flavour between the *Morchella* and the *Helvella*, for both are equally good. Berkeley enumerates four species found in Great Britain; *i.e. H. crispa, lacunosa, elastica*, and *ephippium*. Doubtless all of them would be esculent, but the first two only are large enough or sufficiently plentiful for the table.

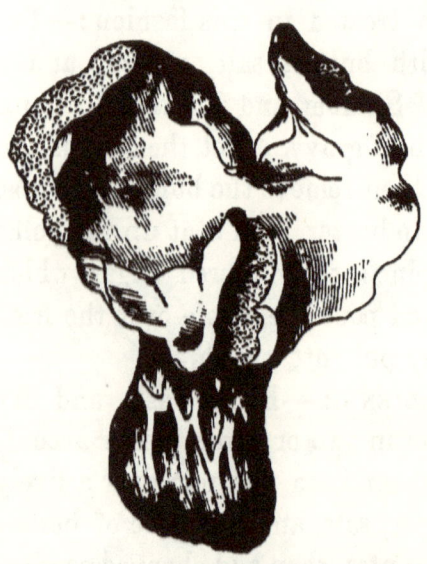

Fig. i.

Helvella crispa has a lobed and deflexed pileus, pallid above and ochraceous beneath (fig. *i*). The stem is fistulose or hollow; when dried, the texture is tough and leathery, and in this condition it resembles crumpled up pieces of wash-leather, that have been saturated with water and allowed to dry. It is a common species in woods, and may occasionally be found growing on banks in the autumn. It is almost impossible to confound these with any other species of fungi found in Britain, so that they may be enjoyed without fear.

Helvella lacunosa is also common, and is found in similar localities to the last. It much resembles *H. crispa* in everything save the colour of the pileus, which, in this instance, is cinereous-black (fig. *k*). This kind is not met with so large or so plentifully as the other. For all purposes to which the morell is applicable, these species may either of them be substituted. They impart an excellent flavour to gravies and soups, and in establishments where they have been once introduced and tested, will, we

Fig. *k*.

doubt not, for ever afterwards hold equal sway with the more aristocratic morell. Unlike the *Agarics*, there is no necessity for the *Helvellas* to be used as soon as gathered, and for this reason, superadded to an experience of their excellent qualities, one can but feel surprised at their absence from our markets

while the truffle and morell obtain at times most ex-
travagant prices. During the past summer a country
gentleman, living remote from town and railway, has
assured us that his own kitchen and those of many of
his friends, are kept with a supply of *Helvellas* for
culinary purposes, from year to year. In Sweden and
Germany they are considered equal to the morell, and
are known in the latter country under the name of
Gemeine morchel or *Stumpf morchel.*

In the succeeding genus, *Verpa*, we meet with forms
somewhat intermediate between the pileate or capped
Helvella and the club-shaped *Geoglossum ;* both species
are, however, rare. The only species of *Spathularia*,
with a yellowish spoon-shaped head, is more common,
as are also two or three of *Geoglossum.* In this genus
the receptacle is club-shaped and simple, with the
fructifying surface surrounding the club, and as our
figure of *G. olivaceum* (Pl. 17) will show, might at first
be taken for a species of *Clavaria.* Both the common
species of this genus are black, and there is no fear of a
tyro cooking them instead of a *Clavaria*, from which
they are further removed by the unbranched and distinctly clubbed termination. One of these is hairy (*G.
hirsutum*) and the other smooth (*G. difforme*), and
both are found growing amongst grass.

The succession of such forms as are met with in the
genus *Peziza* seems to be far more sudden. The cup-
shaped form of the fully expanded plant alone being
considered, it would seem to be out of place ; but its
structural association is far more complete. The genus

is a large one, and the species exceedingly variable in size, some having an expanse of several inches, whilst others are microscopically minute. On account of difference in substance, this genus is subdivided into three series, each of which contains three or four subgenera. Although many of the *Pezizas* are exceedingly beautiful, they are equally useless. It is true that one or two species have been mentioned as affording a wholesome and agreeable article of food, but it is questionable whether they really deserve recommendation. The localities on which these fungi are produced are as variable as they are themselves in colour and size. A great number may be found on the ground, others on damp walls, on the branches and trunks of trees, on stumps and decayed wood, on fir-cones, on plaster ceilings and whitewashed walls, on sticks, rushes, dead leaves, and gravel walks. Of those that are found on wood, the majority confine themselves to trees of one species or genus, whilst a few are less exclusive in their "natural selection."

Allied to this genus is that of *Helotium*, in which the disc, instead of being at first closed as in *Peziza*, is always open: the species are less numerous, but the localities are similar. Nearly all the members of both genera may be collected and dried by exposure to the air, and kept, in company with a little cotton wool that has been dipped in, or sprinkled with, oil of turpentine, in small paper pill-boxes for future reference or examination. Some forms, especially of *Peziza*, resemble the shields or receptacles of certain lichens, with which, nevertheless, none but a novice would confound them.

In the manufacture of the handsome Tunbridge-ware a variety of wood is employed under the name of green oak. Although of a mineral-green colour, this is the ordinary British oak; but the alteration which it has undergone is due to the presence of a fungus. A handsome little species resembling a *Peziza* (*Helotium œruginosum*) traverses with its mycelium the whole fabric of such wood, and these minute threads give their green tint to the timber. When examined under the microscope, the beautiful network of the green mycelium is distinctly seen. This fungus attacks the fallen oak-branches, and the timber affected by it is therefore generally small in diameter; but, from the minute size required in the manufacture for which it is employed, it answers equally with the largest. Green wood is so exceedingly uncommon that, although in a state of decay, the green oak becomes of a marketable value. The little green open cups of this *Helotium* are not so commonly met with as the timber showing traces of its mycelium.

So long since as the time of Pliny and Dioscorides, the truffle seems to have been known and appreciated. There are numerous species, and several of these are indigenous to Britain. In form and habit they differ considerably from the majority of fungi, having the appearance of rough, dark-coloured, warty nodules, occasionally nearly as large as the fist, and which are found buried beneath the surface of the soil (Pl. 23, fig. i.).

The ordinary method of searching for mushrooms will not succeed in this instance, and, therefore, dogs are trained to hunt for truffles by the aid of their peculiar odour, which makes itself evident to the acute canine sense of smell. In some of the continental countries of Europe where these fungi are found, pigs are employed as hunters.

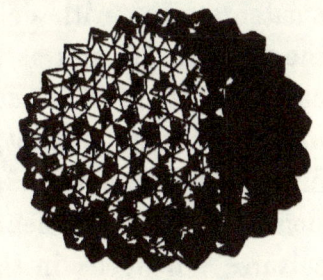

Fig. l.

Kromholz gives the following instructions for the benefit of those who would undertake the search:— " You must have a sow, of five months old, a good walker, with her mouth strapped up, and for her efforts recompense her with acorns ; but as pigs are not easily led, are stubborn, and go astray, and dig after a thousand other things, there is but little to be done with them. Dogs are better ; of these select a small poodle."

The truffle most commonly obtained in Britain is *Tuber æstivum* (the *T. cibarium* of some authors) ; but the ordinary truffles of the Parisian markets are much larger and better flavoured. They are, doubtless, much more common in chalky districts than has been supposed. Our native supplies are obtained chiefly from the downs of Wiltshire, Hampshire, and Kent. From the Continent we import them sliced and dried ; but in this condition one can have but a faint idea of the true truffle flavour, to appreciate which they must be cooked fresh. Lovers of a dish of truffles protest also against the barbarity of paring them, by which process much of the delicious aroma is lost. Like other fungi, these cannot be eaten too fresh; and amateurs speak with delight of fresh truffles cooked in the embers. Inferior as the dried truffles are, they ordinarily realize from fifteen to twenty shillings per pound in the London market, and on the Continent this fungus always obtains a good price, which has occasioned many experiments being made on its artificial culture. In woods in the south of France, truffles are raised by watering the soil with water in which the skins of these tubers have been rubbed. In Vaucluse crops have been raised in a meadow manured with truffle-parings. In the latter locality, also, seedling oaks have been reared, and with them, what have been termed oak-truffles. M. de Gasparin, one of the jurors of the Paris Exposition, has reported the result of his visit to one of these truffle-grounds at Carpentras. Encouraged by the high price of truffles, the proprietor of a somewhat stubborn soil determined to convert it into a truffle-ground. The land was sown with the acorns of the common and of the evergreen oak. In the fourth year three truffles were found, and in about four years more upwards of thirty pounds were collected. When M. de Gasparin visited the plantation, upwards of two pounds of truffles were gathered in a very poor part of the plantation within an hour. All the truffles collected on this ground have been taken at the base of evergreen oaks; but other plantations in Vaucluse produce them at the foot of the common oak. It has been remarked, that the truffles produced about the latter

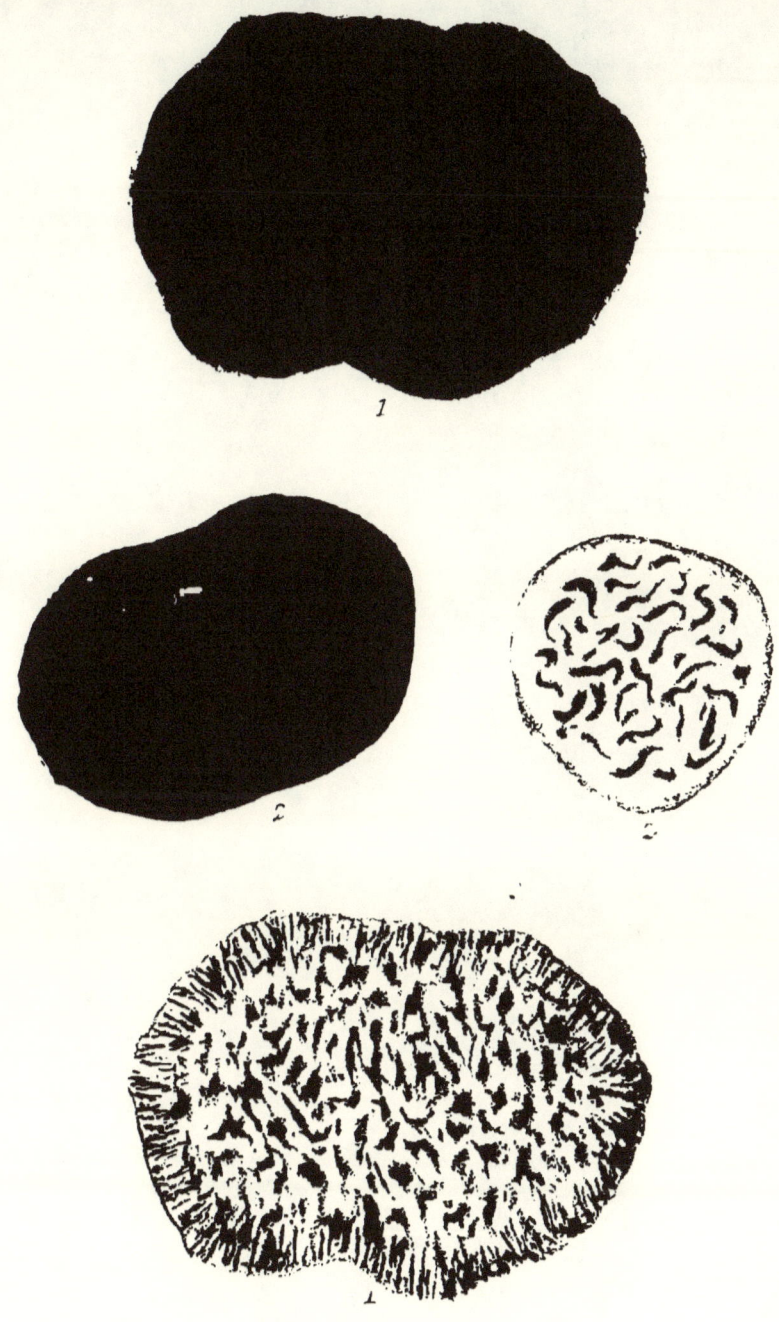

M.C.C. del

1 Tuber æstivum
2 Melanogaster variegatus

E Cooke

trees are larger and more irregular in form than those of the evergreen oak, which are nearly always spherical. The plantation of vines in these truffle-plots has been found advantageous; so that, in some cases, rows of vines alternate with those of oaks. As a remunerative speculation, however, thus far the experiment has not been altogether successful.

M. de Gasparin says, " A sow is employed to search for the truffles. At the distance of twenty feet she scents the truffles and makes rapidly for the foot of the oak, where she finds them, and digs into the earth with her snout. She would soon root up and eat her treasure were she not turned aside by a light stroke of the stick on her nose, and given an acorn or a dry chestnut, which is her reward."

The truffles are gathered at two periods in the year. In May white truffles only are found, which never blacken, and have no odour; these are dried and sold for seasoning. The black truffles are dug up a month before and a month after Christmas, when they have become hard and acquired all their perfume.

In order that all who are fortunate enough to find a dish of fresh truffles may be able to cook them to the best advantage, let us commend them to a few of the most approved methods. If one should desire a *ragoût*, then let the tubers be well washed and afterwards soaked in oil, then cut them in slices about a quarter of an inch in thickness, place them in a stewpan, with oil, or butter if preferred, salt, pepper, and a little white wine. When cooked, bind the whole together with the

yolks of eggs. Another method employed in France
includes a bottle of champagne in the preparation. A
far more economical one consists in wrapping each
truffle in a sheet of buttered paper, and cooking them
by steam. Should it be desired to prepare them *à la
Italienne*, then middle-sized truffles should be selected,
cut into fine slices, placed in a stewpan, with oil, salt,
pepper, parsley, shallots, and chopped garlic. Let them
cook gently over a slow fire, and serve with the juice of
a lemon. If it is preferred that your dish of truffles
should be prepared *à la Piedmontese*, then, having
soaked them in oil, slice them thin, put them in your
stewpan (an eminent French authority says it should
be a silver dish), add thereto salt, oil, and pepper, and
grate over them some Parmesan cheese ; then place the
dish over the hot cinders for a quarter of an hour. One
method which is highly recommended by those who
have adopted it, consists in cleaning some good truffles,
sprinkling them with salt and pepper, and wrapping
them in several folds of paper, garnished with rashers
of bacon. They should be cooked a good hour, then
denuded of their paper envelope, wiped and served hot.
It will suffice to add a method for preparing a *ratifia*
which may recommend itself to some. Take two pounds
of truffles, cut into fragments, and soak them in two
pints of good brandy, to which has been added about
half an ounce of vanilla cut in pieces. After three
weeks, strain the liquor and add two pounds of sugar
dissolved in one pint of water. The *ratifia* may then
be preserved in well-corked bottles for use. If this

process has nothing else to recommend it, it has at least the merit of being rather an expensive one.

Besides this the Rev. M. J. Berkeley states that the following species are also indigenous to Britain : *T. brumale, macrosporum, bituminatum, rufum, scleroneuron, nitidum, puberulum,* and *dryophilum;* but of their esculent properties we confess ourselves profoundly ignorant.

Under the name of *Lycoperdon nuts,* or *Hart's truffles,* one species of *Elaphomyces* (*E. granulatus*) had formerly a medicinal reputation, and might be met with in the herbalists' shops; but now the name is almost unknown. In some country districts, amongst the lovers of the marvellous and antique, it still bears a part of its original reputation, and occasionally obtains employment.

The medicinal substance known under the name of ergot of rye has a fungoid origin, and is, indeed, an altered condition of the grain, caused by the growth of a parasitical species of *Cordiceps* (*C. purpurea*). The mycelium of this parasite traverses the substance of the grain, and so entirely changes its properties, that what was before available as an article of food, now becomes decidedly injurious. Bread made of ergotized grain produces a form of disease called ergotism, which has at different times overspread large districts on the Continent, as though it were the visitation of the plague. The genus *Cordiceps* belongs to the order *Sphæriacei,* which is nearly allied to that which contains the truffle.

DISCRIMINATION AND PRESERVATION OF FUNGI.

It may, perhaps, be anticipated, that some general rules will be given to facilitate discrimination between esculent and poisonous species. Unfortunately all attempts at establishing such a code of regulations, which shall be applicable in all cases, have failed ; for, unless universally applicable, such rules are useless. We remember to have seen the following example of generalization, ·which would exclude several useful species ; viz., "All that have the following characters are poisonous :—

"I. Such as have a cap very thin in proportion to the gills.

"II. Such as have the stalk growing from one side of the cap.

" III. Those in which the gills are all of equal length.

· "IV. Such as have a milky juice.

"V. Such as deliquesce ; that is, run speedily into a dark watery fluid.

"VI. And lastly, every one that has the collar that surrounds the stalk filamentous, or resembling a spider's web."

If the second rule were always true, then the elm agaric, *Agaricus ulmarius,* which has its stem excentric, or near the margin of the cap, would be poisonous, whereas it is often eaten without ill effects. If the fourth rule is without exception, how is it that the orange agaric (*Lactarius deliciosus*), which contains a milky juice, has obtained the name of *delicious*, and is really considered so by those who have tried it, and without inconvenience? If the fifth rule is accepted, then both species of *Coprinus*, which have been recommended as affording an excellent ketchup, must be avoided.

In default, however, of general rules, we would recommend no one to experiment upon species which are unknown to them, or which we have not pointed out as safe. It is not advisable to venture upon such as have a decidedly acrid or unpleasant taste in the raw state, unless they are known to be edible. One or two species which possess such properties when uncooked are wholesome when dressed; but these are exceptions to the general rule. If only such species are employed as we have described in the foregoing pages, and delineated in the plates, there is no fear of unpleasant results. Unfortunately, it is too true that some people will not give themselves the trouble to think or examine, or we should never hear of such manifest stupidity, as confounding the root of monkshood with that of horseradish; two roots almost as unlike as roots well can be, and much more distinct than many a noxious and esculent mushroom. Upon such individuals all rules and recommendations would be thrown away; but the majority of our readers will, we think, confess that we have given them the best guide in the distinct specific characters of each fungus which enjoys a good reputation.

Subject as all fungi are to speedy decomposition, which intimates the existence of new compounds as the result of the chemical action, it is always advisable that all mushrooms, whether of the ordinary kind or those less commonly included under that term, should be prepared for the table as soon as possible after being collected. Not only do they lose flavour by keeping, but they are then more likely to produce unpleasant results. It is also an excellent precaution to employ plenty of salt and spice in the preparation. Even poisonous fungi, and those of an active character, have been cooked with plenty of salt, and eaten with safety. It is only under such circumstances that we can imagine a fungus so injurious as *Amanita muscaria* being eaten at all, as it is said to be in Russia. The fact is equally well known, that in Russia fungi are thoroughly cooked and with plenty of salt. We have always exercised what we believed to be a prudent caution in experimenting upon the esculent qualities of fungi, and would recommend others to follow our example. It is true that we have a number of species which are now known to be wholesome; but an amateur testing a species for the first time would do well to exercise caution in conducting the experiment, to have regard to the taste when raw, and to proceed still more cautiously if there is any evidence of acridity in the uncooked fungus. We would fain hope that our little account will be found a "plain and easy" one, and that it may lead to a better acquaintance with such species as we have recommended without fear; but we would, nevertheless, lend no encouragement to a promiscuous consignment of unknown species to the charge of the cook for a hash or purée.

It has often been alleged, not only that the study of fungi has but few attractions, and cannot compete successfully in interest with that of ferns and algæ, but also that there are such insurmountable obstacles in the way of preserving them, that, having once secured the specimens, there is no chance of making them available for a future occasion. It may be true that the delicate and elegant forms and beautiful tints of many sea-weeds, as well as the graceful outline of the fronds of ferns, may make these members of the vegetable kingdom more suitable for the lady's album, but it is not every one who is privileged to dwell by the seashore through the entire year, and the ferns of one locality may soon be collected and consigned to their resting-places. Fungi, on the contrary, abound everywhere, and the collector can never declare the resources of his locality exhausted. Beautiful objects are by no means rare, and the pocket lens and microscope are sure of constant employment. There is no difficulty whatever in preserving the minute species upon the leaves, or other matrices upon which they vegetate. These may be dried and fastened down upon small squares of white paper, named, and arranged with as great facility as either of the more popular classes of plants to which we have adverted. Occasionally a group will be met with, the individuals composing which are so exceedingly fragile that such a method of preservation will not avail. In many such cases the *mould*, or fungus, may be mounted at once in the ordinary way on a slide for the microscope, and all its features carefully preserved.

The greatest difficulty rests with the larger species, such as many of the *Agarics* and *Boleti*; and for these no better method can be recommended than that detailed by Klotsch, himself an indefatigable collector, thirty years ago:—

"With a delicate scimitar-shaped knife or scalpel, such as is found in a surgeon's instrument·case, I make a double vertical section, through the middle, from the top of the pileus to the base of·the stem, so as to remove a slice. This, it will be at once seen, shows the vertical outline of the whole fungus, the internal nature of its stem, whether hollow, or spongy, or solid, the thickness of the pileus, and the peculiarities of the gills, whether equal or unequal in length, decurrent upon the stem, or otherwise, &c. There will then remain the two sides, or nearly halves of the fungus, which each in itself gives a correct idea, if I may so express myself, of the whole circumference of the plant. But before we proceed to dry them, it is necessary to separate the stem from the pileus, and from the latter to scrape out the fleshy lamellæ or gills, if an *Agaric*, or the tubes of a *Boletus*. We have thus the fungus divided into five portions,—a central thin slice, two nearly halves of the stem, and the same sections of the pileus. These, after being a little exposed to the air, that they may part with some of their moisture, but not so long that they shrivel, are to be placed between dry blotting-paper, and subjected to pressure as other plants, the papers being changed daily till the specimens are per-fectly dry. When this is the case, the central portion or slice and the two halves of the stem are to be fastened upon white paper, together with the respective halves of the pileus upon the top of the latter in their original position. Here will thus be three sections from which a correct idea of the whole plant may be obtained. The *volva* and *ring* of such species as possess them must be retained. With care, even the most fugacious species may be well preserved, according to this method. Some of the smaller and less fleshy kinds will not require to have the gills removed. In collecting fleshy fungi, care must be taken that they are not too old, and absolutely in a state of decomposition, or too much infested with the larvæ of insects. When this latter is the case, some oil of turpentine poured over them will either drive them rapidly from their holes, or destroy them. Species with a clammy viscid pileus it is better to expose to a dry air or the heat of a fire, before being placed in papers.

" The separate parts of the genera *phallus* and *clathrus* I fill with cotton, keep them for a time exposed to a dry atmosphere, and then, after removing the cotton, subject them to pressure. The same may be done with the large tremelloid *Pezizæ*."

In order to protect the specimens as far as possible from insects, it is recommended that they should be washed over, by the aid of a camel-hair pencil, with oil of turpentine, in which a little finely powdered corrosive sublimate has been mixed. As the sublimate will not dissolve in the turpentine, it is essential that it should be powdered as fine as possible, and that the mixture should be well shaken before it is employed.

Some of the smaller species may be dried at once without dissection, and there are others, which, though larger, are less watery, and may be dried in a current of air, so as to retain much of their original character. Many of the species of *Polyporus*, *Dædalea*, *Thelephora*, &c., require nothing more than drying in the air, washing with a little turpentine, and keeping in paper trays or boxes. It is scarce worthy of inquiry what fluid will best preserve the specimens immersed in it, since the room occupied by a series of glass bottles or jars, each containing its own individual species, would be so great as to render the method impracticable. Withering recommended that for such a process two ounces of sulphate of copper should be powdered and dissolved in a pint of boiling water, and when cold added to half a pint of spirits of wine. In this liquor the specimens should be immersed for three or four hours, then taken out and placed permanently in glass bottles containing a preserving fluid of the proportions of three fluid ounces of spirits of wine to a pint of water. We nevertheless entertain serious doubts whether such a plan would in its results offer compensation for the labour, room, and expense to be sacrificed.

TABULAR ARRANGEMENT

of

BRITISH FUNGI.

——◦——

CELLULAR flowerless plants, nourished through their mycelium or spawn; living in air; propagated by spores; naked, or inclosed in asci. Destitute of green gonidia (by which feature they are distinguished from LICHENS).

COHORT I.—SPORIFERI.

Having the spores or reproductive bodies naked or exposed.

Family I.
HYMENOMYCETES or AGARICACEÆ.

Hymenium, or spore-bearing surface, exposed; spores generally in fours, borne on distinct spicules.

Order I.—AGARICINI. *Gill-bearing Fungi.*

Hymenium, or spore-bearing surface, inferior, spread over lamellæ or gills, which radiate from a common centre, and each of which may be separated into two plates.

Genera.

AMANITA. Volva distinct; gills membranaceous, persistent, acute.

12 British species.

AGARICUS, *L.* Gills membranaceous, not melting; edge acute.

Series 1.—*Leucospori*, with white spores.

Sub-Gen. Lepiota.	Sub-Gen. Collybia.
Armillaria.	Mycena.
Tricholoma.	Omphalia.
Clitocybe.	Pleurotus.
	190 *British species.*

Series 2. — *Hyporhodii*, with salmon-coloured spores.

Volvaria.	Leptonia.
Pluteus.	Nolanea.
Entoloma.	Eccilia.
Clitopilus.	41 *Brit. sp.*

Series 3.—*Dermini*, with ferruginous spores, sometimes tawny.

Pholiota.	Naucoria.
Hebeloma.	Galera.
Flammula.	Crepidotus.
	78 *Brit. sp.*

Series 4.—*Pratellœ*, with brownish-purple or brown spores.

Psalliota.	Psilocybo.
Hypholoma.	Psathyra.
	44 *Brit. sp.*

Series 5.—*Coprinarii*, with black spores.

| Panæolus. | Psathyrella. |
| | 14 *Brit. sp.* |

COPRINUS, *Fr.* Gills membranaceous, deliquescent; spores black.

28 *Brit. sp.*

BOLBITIUS, *Fr.* Gills becoming moist; spores coloured.

4 *Brit. sp.*

CORTINARIUS, *Fr.* Gills persistent; veil arachnoid or cobweb-like; spores rusty ochre.

Sub-Gen. Phlegmacium.	Sub-Gen. Dermocybe.
Myxacium.	Telamonia.
Inoloma.	Hygrocybe.
	51 *Brit. sp.*

PAXILLUS, *Fr.* Gills persistent, distinct from hymenophorum.

3 *Brit. sp.*

GOMPHIDIUS, *Fr.* Gills slightly branched ; pileus top-
shaped ; spores fusiform.

3 *Brit. sp.*

HYGROPHORUS, *Fr.* Hymenophorum continuous with
stem.

29 *Brit. sp.*

LACTARIUS, *Fr.* Gills milky. .

28 *Brit. sp.*

RUSSULA, *Fr.* Gills rigid, not milky ; veil 0.

24 *Brit. sp.*

CANTHARELLUS, *Fr.* Gills thick, branched, obtuse-edged.

10 *Brit. sp.*

NYCTALIS, *Fr.* Gills fleshy, obtuse ; often parasitic.

2 *Brit. sp.*

MARASMIUS, *Fr.* Hymenium dry, continuous between the
gills ; lamellæ thick, rough, and acute-edged.

25 *Brit. sp.*

LENTINUS, *Fr.* Pileus hard, dry, and tough ; edge of gills
acute, toothed.

7 *Brit. sp.*

PANUS, *Fr.* Pileus fleshy and tough ; edge acute, entire.

3 *Brit. sp.*

XEROTUS, *Fr.* Gills tough and forked ; edge obtuse,
entire.

1 *Brit. sp.*

SCHIZOPHYLLUM, *Fr.* Gills split longitudinally, with the
two divisions spreading.

1 *Brit. sp.*

LENZITES, *Fr.* Corky ; gills anastomosing.

4 *Brit. sp.*

Order II.—POLYPOREI. *Tube-bearing Fungi.*

Hymenium, or spore-bearing surface, lining the cavities of tubes or pores, which are sometimes broken up into plates.

Genera.

BOLETUS, *Fr.* Tubes separable from one another ; hymenophorum distinct from hymenium.

31 *Brit. sp.*

STROBILOMYCES, *Berk.* Spores globose, or broadly elliptic and rough.

1 *Brit. sp.*

POLYPORUS, *Fr.* Pores not easily separable.

78 *Brit. sp.*

TRAMETES, *Fr.* Pores concrete with the pileus.

4 *Brit. sp.*

DÆDALEA, *Pers.* Corky ; pores labyrinthiform.

4 *Brit. sp.*

MERULIUS, *Fr.* Waxy, with sinuous toothed folds.

10 *Brit. sp.*

POROTHELIUM, *Fr.* Covered with papillæ, ultimately opening.

· 1 *Brit. sp.*

FISTULINA, *Bull.* Hymenium inferior ; papillæ forming distinct tubes.

1 *Brit. sp.*

Order III.—HYDNEI. *Spine-bearing Fungi.*

Fructifying surface spread over spines or teeth.

Genera.

HYDNUM, *L.* Spines awl-shaped, distinct.

23 *Brit. sp.*

SISTOTREMA, *Pers.* Gill-like teeth, irregularly distributed, bearing the hymenium.

1 *Brit. sp.*

IRPEX, *Fr.* Teeth in rows, or like network connected.

3 *Brit. sp.*

RADULUM, *Fr.* With waxy irregular tubercles.

2 *Brit. sp.*

PHLEBIA, *Fr.* Hymenium subgelatinous, spread over persistent veins.

4 *Brit. sp.*

GRANDINIA, *Fr.* Hymenium granulated.

1 *Brit. sp.*

ODONTIA, *Fr.* With spiny, crested warts.

1 *Brit. sp.*

KNEIFFIA, *Fr.* Hymenium rough, with bristles.

1 *Brit. sp.*

Order IV.—AURICULARINI. *Leathery Fungi.*
Hymenium commonly even.

Genera.

CRATERELLUS, *Fr.*	AURICULARIA, *Fr.*
4 *Brit. sp.*	2 *Brit. sp.*
THELEPHORA, *Fr.*	CORTICIUM, *Fr.*
19 *Brit. sp.*	23 *Brit. sp.*
STEREUM, *Fr.*	CYPHELLA, *Fr.*
6 *Brit. sp.*	11 *Brit. sp.*
HYMENOCHÆTE, *Lév.*	
3 *Brit. sp.*	

Order V.—CLAVARIEI. *Club-bearing Fungi.*

The hymenium not confined to a particular surface, and scarcely distinct ; vertical.

Genera.

CLAVARIA, *L.*	TYPHULA, *Fr.*
32 *Brit. sp.*	7 *Brit. sp.*
CALOCERA, *Fr.*	PISTILLARIA, *Fr.*
4 *Brit. sp.*	5 *Brit. sp.*

K

Order VI.—TREMELLINI. *Gelatinous Fungi.*

Whole plant gelatinous ; spicules elongated threads.

Genera.

TREMELLA, *Fr.*
17 *Brit. sp.*

EXIDIA, *Fr.*
3 *Brit. sp.*

HIRNEOLA, *Fr.*
1 *Brit. sp.*

NŒMATELLA, *Fr.*
3 *Brit. sp.*

DACRYMYCES, *Nees.*
4 *Brit. sp.*

APYRENIUM, *Fr.*
1 *Brit. sp.*

HYMENULA, *Fr.*
1 *Brit. sp.*

DITIOLA, *Fr.*
1 *Brit. sp.*

———

Family II.

GASTEROMYCETES or LYCOPERDACEÆ.

Hymenium, or spore-bearing surface, enclosed in a peridium ; spores generally in fours, on distinct spicules or stalks.

Order VII.—HYPOGÆI. *Subterranean Fungi.*

Hymenium not becoming dusty, or melting ; subterranean.

Genera.

OCTAVIANIA, *Vitt.*
2 *Brit. sp.*

MELANOGASTER, *Corda.*
2 *Brit. sp.*

HYDNANGIUM, *Wallr.*
1 *Brit. sp.*

HYSTERANGIUM, *Vitt.*
2 *Brit. sp.*

RHIZOPOGON, *Tul.*
1 *Brit. sp.*

HYMENOGASTER, *Tul.*
11 *Brit. sp.*

Order VIII—PHALLOIDEI. *Stinkhorn Fungi.*
Hymenium melting.

Genera.

PHALLUS, *L.*
    2 *Brit. sp.*
CYNOPHALLUS, *Fr.*
    1 *Brit. sp.*

CLATHRUS, *Mich.*
    1 *Brit. sp.*

Order IX.—TRICHOGASTRES. *Puff-ball Fungi.*
Hymenium drying into a dusty mass.

Genera.

BATARREA, *Pers.*
    1 *Brit. sp.*
TULOSTOMA, *Pers.*
    1 *Brit. sp.*
GEASTER, *Mich.*
    9 *Brit. sp.*
BOVISTA, *Dill.*
    2 *Brit. sp.*

LYCOPERDON, *Tourn.*
    7 *Brit. sp.*
SCLERODERMA, *Pers.*
    8 *Brit. sp.*
POLYSACCUM, *D. C.*
    1 *Brit. sp.*
CENOCOCCUM, *Fr.*
    1 *Brit. sp.*

Order X.—MYXOGASTRES. *Dust Fungi.*

At first pulpy; afterwards filled with threads and dust-like spores.

Genera.

LYCOGALA, *Mich.*
    2 *Brit. sp.*
RETICULARIA, *Bull.*
    3 *Brit. sp.*

ÆTHALIUM, *Link.*
    2 *Brit. sp.*
SPUMARIA *Pers*
    1 *Brit. sp.*

K 2

DIDERMA, *Pers.*
　　　　13 *Brit. sp.*

DIDYMIUM, *Schrad.*
　　　　17 *Brit. sp.*

PHYSARUM, *Pers.*
　　　　·7 *Brit. sp.*

ANGIORIDIUM, *Grev.*
　　　　1 *Brit. sp.*

BADHAMIA, *Berk.*
　　　　5 *Brit. sp.*

CRATERIUM, *Trent.*
　　　　5 *Brit. sp.*

DIACHEA, *Fr.*
　　　　1 *Brit. sp.*

STEMONITIS, *Gled.*
　　　　9 *Brit. sp.*

ENERTHENEMA, *Bowm.*
　　　　1 *Brit. sp.*

DICTYDIUM, *Schrad.*
　　　　1 *Brit. sp.*

CRIBRARIA, *Schrad.*
　　　　2 *Brit. sp.*

ARCYRIA, *Hill.*
　　　　6 *Brit. sp.*

OPHIOTHECA, *Curr.*
　　　　1 *Brit. sp.*

TRICHIA, *Hall.*
　　　　13 *Brit. sp.*

PERICHÆNA, *Fr.*
　　　　2 *Brit. sp.*

LICEA, *Schrad.*
　　　　4 *Brit. sp.*

PHELONITIS, *Chev.*
　　　　1 *Brit. sp.*

Order XI.—NIDULARIACEI.　*Nest-bearing Fungi.*

Spores compacted into globose or disk-shaped bodies, nested in a distinct peridium.

Genera.

CYATHUS, *Pers.*
　　　　2 *Brit. sp.*

CRUCIBULUM, *Tul.*
　　　　1 *Brit. sp.*

SPHÆROBALUS, *Tode.*
　　　　1 *Brit. sp.*

THELEBOLUS, *Tode.*
　　　　1 *Brit. sp.*

POLYANGIUM, *Link.*
　　　　1 *Brit. sp.*

Family III.
CONIOMYCETES or UREDINACEÆ.

Spores single, on more or less distinct sporophores; flocci, or threads of the fruit, obsolete, or nearly so.

Order XII.—SPHÆRONEMEI.
Perithecium distinct.

Genera.

CONIOTHYRIUM, *Corda.*
1 *Brit. sp.*

LEPTOSTROMA, *Fr.*
6 *Brit. sp.*

PHOMA, *Fr.*
22 *Brit. sp.*

LEPTOTHYRIUM, *Kze.*
3 *Brit. sp.*

ACTINOTHYRIUM, *Kze.*
1 *Brit. sp.*

CRYPTOSPORIUM, *Kze.*
2 *Brit. sp.*

SPHÆRONEMA, *Tode.*
4 *Brit. sp.*

APOSPHÆRIA, *Berk.*
2 *Brit. sp.*

SPHÆROPSIS, *Lév.*
15 *Brit. sp.*

DOTHIORA, *Fr.*
2 *Brit. sp.*

CLINTERIUM, *Fr.*
1 *Brit. sp.*

ACROSPERMUM, *Tode.*
2 *Brit. sp.*

DIPLODIA, *Fr.*
14 *Brit. sp.*

HENDERSONIA, *Berk.*
8 *Brit. sp.*

DARLUCA, *Cast.*
3 *Brit. sp.*

VERMICULARIA, *Tode.*
4 *Brit. sp.*

DISCOSIA, *Lib.*
1 *Brit. sp.*

PILIDIUM, *Kze.*
2 *Brit. sp.*

MELASMIA, *Lév.*
2 *Brit. sp.*

PIGGOTIA, *Berk.*
1 *Brit. sp.*

SEPTORIA, *Fr.*
22 *Brit. sp.*

ASCOCHYTA, *Lib.*
4 *Brit. sp.*

CYSTOTRICHA, *Berk.*
1 *Brit. sp.*

NEOTTIOSPORIA, *Desm.*
1 *Brit. sp.*

EXCIPULA, *Fr.*
4 *Brit. sp.*

DINEMASPORIUM, *Lév.*
1 *Brit. sp.*

MYXORMIA, *Berk.*
1 *Brit. sp.*

PROSTHEMIUM, *Kze.*
2 *Brit. sp.*

ASTEROMA, *D. C.*
6 *Brit. sp.*

RABENHORSTIA, *Fr.*
2 *Brit. sp.*

CYTISPORA, *Fr.*
8 *Brit. sp.*

MICROPERA, *Lév.*
1 *Brit. sp.*

DISCELLA, *Berk.*
5 *Brit. sp.*

PHLYCTÆNA, *Desm.*
2 *Brit. sp.*

CEUTHOSPORA, *Fr.*
2 *Brit. sp.*

ERIOSPORA, *Berk.*
1 *Brit. sp.*

Order XIII.—MELANCONIEI.

Perithecium obsolete or absent.

Genera.

MELANCONIUM, *Link.*
3 *Brit. sp.*

STEGONOSPORIUM, *Corda.*
1 *Brit. sp.*

STILBOSPORA, *Pers.*
2 *Brit. sp.*

ASTEROSPORIUM, *Kze.*
1 *Brit. sp.*

CORYNEUM, *Kze.*
6 *Brit. sp.*

PESTALOZZIA, *De Not.*
1 *Brit. sp.*

CHEIROSPORA, *Fr.*
1 *Brit. sp.*

NEMASPORA, *Pers.*
2 *Brit. sp.*

MYXOSPORIUM, *De Not.*
3 *Brit. sp.*

GLÆOSPORIUM, *Mont.*
4 *Brit. sp.*

Order XIV.—TORULACEI.

Perithecium obsolete ; fructifying surface naked.

Genera.

TORULA, *Pers.*	SPORIDESMIUM, *Link.*
12 *Brit. sp.*	8 *Brit. sp.*
BACTRIDIUM, *Kze.*	CONIOTHECIUM, *Corda.*
3 *Brit. sp.*	2 *Brit. sp.*
HELICOSPORIUM, *Nees.*	DICTYOSPORIUM, *Corda.*
2 *Brit. sp.*	1 *Brit. sp.*
BISPORA, *Corda.*	TETRAPLOA, *Berk.*
1 *Brit. sp.*	1 *Brit. sp.*
SEPTONEMA, *Corda.*	ECHINOBOTRYUM, *Corda.*
2 *Brit. sp.*	1 *Brit. sp.*
SPOROSCHISMA, *Berk.*	GYMNOSPORIUM, *Corda.*
1 *Brit. sp.*	1 *Brit. sp.*

Order XV.—PUCCINIÆI. *Parasitic or Mildew Fungi.*

Peridium obsolete ; spores germinating, and producing secondary spores.

Genera.

XENODOCHUS, *Schlecht.*	PODISOMA, *Link.*
1 *Brit. sp.*	3 *Brit. sp.*
AREGMA, *Fr.*	UREDO, *Lév.*
5 *Brit. sp.*	13 *Brit. sp.*
TRIPHRAGMIUM, *Link.*	TRICHOBASIS, *Lév.*
1 *Brit. sp.*	25 *Brit. sp.*
PUCCINIA, *Pers.*	UROMYCES, *Lév.*
42 *Brit. sp.*	9 *Brit. sp.*
GYMNOSPORANGIUM, *D. C.*	COLEOSPORIUM, *Lév.*
1 *Brit. sp.*	6 *Brit. sp.*

MELAMPSORA, *Cast.*

    5 *Brit. sp.*

LECYTHEA, *Lév.*

    12 *Brit. sp.*

CYSTOPUS, *Lév.*

    1 *Brit. sp.*

POLYCYSTES, *Lév.*

    3 *Brit. sp.*

TILLETIA, *Tul.*

    1 *Brit. sp.*

USTILAGO, *Link.*

    15 *Brit. sp.*

TUBURCINIA, *Fr.*

    2 *Brit. sp.*

Order XVI.—ÆCIDIACEI.

Peridium cellular.

Genera.

RŒSTELIA, *Reb.*

    3 *Brit. sp.*

PERIDERMIUM, *Chev.*

    2 *Brit. sp.*

ÆCIDIUM, *Pers.*

    30 *Brit. sp.*

EUDOPHYLLUM, *Lév.*

    1 *Brit. sp.*

Family IV.

HYPHOMYCETES or BOTRYACEÆ.

Filamentous ; spores naked, often with divisions.

Order XVII.—ISARIACEI.

Threads compacted.

Genera.

ISARIA, *Hill.*

    Brit. sp.

AUTHINA, *Fr.*

    1 *Brit. sp.*

CERATIUM, *A. and S.*

    1 *Brit. sp.*

PACHNOCYBE, *Berk.*

    4 *Brit. sp.*

Order XVIII.—STILBACEI.

Receptacle globose ; spores minute, involved in gluten.

Genera.

STILBUM, *Tode.*
14 *Brit. sp.*
ATRACTIUM, *Fr.*
1 *Brit. sp.*
VOLUTELLA, *Tode.*
5 *Brit. sp.*
TUBERCULARIA, *Tode.*
4 *Brit. sp.*
FUSARIUM, *Link.*
4 *Brit. sp.*

MYROTHECIUM, *Tode.*
1 *Brit. sp.*
EPICOCCUM, *Link.*
2 *Brit. sp.*
ILLOSPORIUM, *Mart.*
4 *Brit. sp.*
ÆGERITA, *Pers.*
1 *Brit. sp.*

Order XIX.—DEMATIEI. *Black Moulds.*

Threads free, coated, or dark-coloured ; never white.

Genera.

ARTHROBOTRYUM, *Cesati.*
2 *Brit. sp.*
DENDRYPHIUM, *Corda.*
5 *Brit. sp.*
PERICONIA, *Corda.*
2 *Brit. sp.*
SPOROCYBE, *Fr.*
3 *Brit. sp.*
STACHYBOTRYS, *Corda.*
2 *Brit. sp.*
HAPLOGRAPHIUM, *Berk.*
1 *Brit. sp.*

MONOTOSPORA, *Corda.*
2 *Brit. sp.*
CEPHALOTRICHUM, *Link.*
1 *Brit. sp.*
ŒDEMIUM, *Fr.*
1 *Brit. sp.*
HELMINTHOSPORIUM, *Link.*
20 *Brit. sp.*
MYSTROSPORIUM, *Corda.*
1 *Brit. sp.*
MACROSPORIUM, *Fr.*
4 *Brit. sp.*

TRIPOSPORIUM, *Corda.*
: 1 *Brit. sp.*

HELICOMA, *Corda.*
: 1 *Brit. sp.*

CLADOTRICHUM, *Corda.*
: 1 *Brit. sp.*

POLYTHRINCIUM, *Kze.*
: 1 *Brit. sp.*

CLADOSPORIUM, *Link.*
: 6 *Brit. sp.*

ARTHRINIUM, *Kze.*
: 1 *Brit. sp.*

GONATOSPORIUM, *Corda.*
: 1 *Brit. sp.*

CAMPTOUM, *Link.*
: 1 *Brit. sp.*

SPORODUM, *Corda.*
: 1 *Brit. sp.*

Order XX.—MUCEDINES. *Blue Moulds.*
Threads never coated, white or coloured.

Genera.

ASPERGILLUS, *Mich.*
: 6 *Brit. sp.*

NEMATOGONUM, *Desm.*
: 2 *Brit. sp.*

RHINOTRICHUM, *Corda.*
: 3 *Brit. sp.*

BOTRYTIS, *Mich.*
: 4 *Brit. sp.*

PERONOSPORA, *Corda.*
: 14 *Brit. sp.*

VERTICILLIUM, *Link.*
: 4 *Brit. sp.*

HAPLARIA, *Link.*
: 1 *Brit. sp.*

POLYACTIS, *Link.*
: 5 *Brit. sp.*

PENICILLIUM, *Link.*
: 6 *Brit. sp.*

OIDIUM, *Link.*
: 10 *Brit. sp.*

CYLINDRIUM, *Bon.*
: 1 *Brit. sp.*

MONILIA, *Hill.*
: 2 *Brit. sp.*

DACTYLIUM, *Nees.*
: 8 *Brit. sp.*

FUSIDIUM, *Link.*
: 3 *Brit. sp.*

SPOROTRICHUM, *Link.*
: 6 *Brit. sp.*

ZYGODESMUS, *Corda.*
: 1 *Brit. sp.*

VIRGARIA, *Nees.*
: 1 *Brit. sp.*

BOLACOTRICHA, *Berk.*
: 1 *Brit. sp.*

MYXOTRICHUM, *Kze.*
: 2 *Brit. sp.*

GONYTRICHUM, *Nees.*
: 1 *Brit. sp.*

MENISPORA, *Pers.*
1 *Brit. sp.*
CHÆTOPSIS, *Grev.*
1 *Brit. sp.*
ACREMONIUM, *Link.*
3 *Brit. sp.*
GONATOBOTRYS, *Corda.*
1 *Brit. sp.*

CLONOSTACHYS, *Corda.*
1 *Brit. sp.*
BOTRYOSPORIUM, *Corda.*
2 *Brit. sp.*
PAPULASPORA, *Preuss.*
1 *Brit. sp.*
RHOPALOMYCES, *Corda.*
2 *Brit. sp.*

Order XXI.—SEPEDONIEI.

Mycelium threadlike ; spores resting on the matrix.

Genera.

SEPEDONIUM, *Link.*
2 *Brit. sp.*
FUSISPORIUM, *Link.*
10 *Brit. sp.*
EPOCHNIUM, *Link.*
1 *Brit. sp.*

PSILONIA, *Fr.*
3 *Brit. sp.*
ACROSPEIRA, *Berk.*
1 *Brit. sp.*

Order XXII.—TRICHODERMACEI.

Threads covering the spores with a kind of peridium.

Genera.

PILACRE, *Fr.*
2 *Brit. sp.*
INSTITALE, *Fr.*
1 *Brit. sp.*

TRICHODERMA, *Pers.*
1 *Brit. sp.*
ARTHRODERMA, *Curr.*
1 *Brit. sp.*

Cohort II.—SPORIDIIFERA.

Having the spores or reproductive bodies contained in asci or bags.

Family V.
PHYSOMYCETES or MUCORACEÆ.

Spores surrounded by a veil or sporangium.

Order XXIII.—ANTENNARIEI.
Threads black, felted, moniliform.

Genera.

ANTENNARIA, *Link.*
1 *Brit. sp.*

ZASMIDIUM, *Fr.*
1 *Brit. sp.*

Order XXIV.—MUCORINI.
Threads free, bearing sporangia.

Genera.

ASCOPHORA, *Tode.*
2 *Brit. sp.*

MUCOR, *Mich.*
11 *Brit. sp.*

HYDROPHORA, *Tode.*
1 *Brit. sp.*

ENDODROMIA, *Berk.*
1 *Brit. sp.*

SPORODINIA, *Link.*
1 *Brit. sp.*

ACROSTALAGMUS, *Corda.*
1 *Brit. sp.*

SYZYGITES, *Ehrenb.*
1 *Brit. sp.*

EUDOGONE, *Link.*
2 *Brit. sp.*

Family VI.

ASCOMYCETES or HELVELLACEÆ.

Sporidia generally eight together, contained in a case or ascus.

Order XXV.—ELVELLACEI.

Substance soft ; hymenium at length exposed.

Genera.

MORCHELLA, *Dill.*
3 *Brit. sp.*

GYROMITRA, *Fr.*
1 *Brit. sp.*

HELVELLA, *Link.*
4 *Brit. sp.*

VERPA, *Schwartz.*
2 *Brit. sp.*

MITRULA, *Fr.*
2 *Brit. sp.*

PEZIZA, *Link.*

SPATHULARIA, *Pers.*
1 *Brit. sp.*

LEOTIA, *Hill.*
2 *Brit. sp.*

VIBRISSEA, *Fr.*
1 *Brit. sp.*

GEOGLOSSUM, *Pers.*
6 *Brit. sp.*

Series 1.—*Aleuria,* Fleshy ; cup always open.
Sub-Gen. Discina.   *Sub-Gen.* Humaria.
Geopyxis.   Encælia.

Series 2.—*Lachnea,* Waxy ; cups hairy.
Sarcoscypha.   Tapesia.
Dasyscyphæ.   Fibrina.

Series 3.—*Phialea,* Waxy, or membranaceous ; cups
smooth.
Hymenoscypha.   Patellea.
Mollisia.
133 *Brit. sp.*

HELOTIUM, *Fr.*
35 *Brit. sp.*

PSILOPEZIA, *Berk.*
1 *Brit. sp.*

PATELLARIA, *Fr.*
7 *Brit. sp.*

SPHINCTRINA, *Fr.*
1 *Brit. sp.*

LAQUEARIA, *Fr.*
  1 *Brit. sp.*
TYMPANIS, *Tode.*
  4 *Brit. sp.*
CENANGIUM, *Fr.*
  9 *Brit. sp.*
ASCOBOLUS, *Tode.*
  7 *Brit. sp.*

BULGARIA, *Fr.*
  2 *Brit. sp.*
AGYRIUM, *Fr.*
  1 *Brit. sp.*
STICTIS, *Pers.*
  12 *Brit. sp.*
ASCOMYCES, *Mont. & Desm.*
  4 *Brit. sp.*

Order XXVI.—TUBERACEI.

Subterranean ; hymenium wavy and packed.

Genera.

TUBER, *Mich.*
  9 *Brit. sp.*
CHOIROMYCES, *Vitt.*
  1 *Brit. sp.*
AMYLOCARPUS, *Curr.*
  1 *Brit. sp.*
PACHYPHLŒUS, *Tul.*
  3 *Brit. sp.*
STEPHENSIA, *Tul.*
  1 *Brit. sp.*
HYDNOTRYA, *Berk.*
  1 *Brit. sp.*

HYDNOBOLITES, *Tul.*
  1 *Brit. sp.*
SPHÆROSOMA, *Kl.*
  1 *Brit. sp.*
BALSAMIA, *Vitt.*
  1 *Brit. sp.*
GENEA, *Vitt.*
  3 *Brit. sp.*
ELAPHOMYCES, *Nees.*
  3 *Brit. sp.*

Order XXVII.—PHACIDIACEI.

Hard ; hymenium ultimately exposed.

Genera.

PHACIDIUM, *Fr.*
  8 *Brit. sp.*
HETEROSPHÆRIA, *Grev.*
  1 *Brit. sp.*

RHYTISMA, *Fr.*
  6 *Brit. sp.*
TRIBLIDIUM, *Reb.*
  1 *Brit. sp.*

HYSTERIUM, *Tode.*

17 *Brit. sp.*

AILOGRAPHUM, *Lib.*

2 *Brit. sp.*

ASTERINA, *Lév.*

1 *Brit. sp.*

LOPHIUM, *Fr.*

2 *Brit. sp.*

STEGIA, *Fr.*

1 *Brit. sp.*

TROCHILA, *Fr.*

2 *Brit. sp.*

Order XXVIII.—SPHÆRIACEI.

Perithecia opening by a distinct ostiolum or orifice.

Genera.

CORDICEPS, *Fr.*

10 *Brit. sp.*

HYPOCREA, *Fr.*

11 *Brit. sp.*

ENDOTHIA, *Fr.*

1 *Brit. sp.*

XYLARIA, *Schrank.*

7 *Brit. sp.*

THAMNOMYCES, *Ehrb.*

1 *Brit. sp.*

PORONIA, *Fr.*

1 *Brit. sp.*

HYPOXYLON, *Bull.*

17 *Brit. sp.*

DIATRYPE, *Fr.*

33 *Brit. sp.*

VALSA, *Fr.*

51 *Brit. sp.*

MELOGRAMMA, *Fr.*

4 *Brit. sp.*

DOTHIDEA, *Fr.*

17 *Brit. sp.*

ISOTHEA, *Fr.*

3 *Brit. sp.*

HYPOSPILA, *Fr.*

2 *Brit. sp.*

STIGMATEA, *Fr.*

7 *Brit. sp.*

OOMYCES, *Berk. & Br.*

1 *Brit. sp.*

NECTRIA, *Fr.*

26 *Brit. sp.*

SPHÆRIA, *Hall.*

215 *Brit. sp.*

CERATOSTOMA, *Fr.*

2 *Brit. sp.*

MASSARIA, *De Not.*

3 *Brit. sp.*

HERCOSPORA, *Fr.*

1 *Brit. sp.*

PYRENOPHORA, *Fr.*

    1 *Brit. sp.*

GIBBERA, *Fr.*

    3 *Brit. sp.*

DICHÆNA, *Fr.*

    2 *Brit. sp.*

CAPNODIUM, *Mont.*

    1 *Brit. sp.*

Order XXIX.—PERISPORIACEI.

Perithecia free, often surrounded by threads; asci springing from the base.

Genera.

PERISPORIUM, *Fr.*

    2 *Brit. sp.*

LASIOBOTRYS, *Kze.*

    2 *Brit. sp.*

SPHÆROTHECA, *Lév.*

    2 *Brit. sp.*

PHYLLACTINIA, *Lév.*

    1 *Brit. sp.*

UNCINULA, *Lév.*

    2 *Brit. sp.*

MICROSPHÆRA, *Lév.*

    3 *Brit. sp.*

ERYSIPHE, *Hedw.*

    7 *Brit. sp.*

CHÆTOMIUM, *Kze.*

    3 *Brit. sp.*

ASCOTRICHA, *Berk.*

    1 *Brit. sp.*

EUROTIUM, *Link.*

    1 *Brit. sp.*

Order XXX.—ONYGENEI.

Peridium of closely woven threads; sporidia in a compact dusty mass.

Genus.

ONYGENA, *Pers.*

    3 *Brit. sp.*

INDEX.

L

ROBERT HARDWICKE, PRINTER, 192, PICCADILLY.

By the same Author,

A MANUAL

OF

BOTANICAL TERMS,

FOR THE

USE OF SCHOOLS, CLASSES, AND PRIVATE STUDENTS.

WITH UPWARDS OF 300 WOODCUTS.

Fcap. 8vo, pricè 2s. 6d.

Critic.

"This elegant little volume will be a welcome boon to all botanical students. It contains intelligible descriptions of all the terms used in botanical science, with a collection of beautifully-executed illustrations at the end of the volume. To all who do not, but are willing to know the full meaning of such terms as Campylospermous, Sterigmate, and Perichætium, this volume may be safely recommended."

Mining Journal.

"In a small volume, comprising only 90 pages of letter-press, and illustrated with two dozen plates, Mr. Cooke has given a complete glossary of all the technicalities of the science in present use; and we do not hesitate to say that, by the careful use of the book, a sound knowledge of the theoretical portion of Botany may be obtained, without tedious labour from any standard work upon the subject."

The Dial.

"This book affords special facilities for the acquisition of the technicalities of botanical science to such as are not already masters of the dead languages. It is illustrated by numerous explanatory diagrams."

LONDON: ROBERT HARDWICKE, 192, PICCADILLY, W.

BY THE SAME AUTHOR,

Price One Shilling; bound in cloth, Eighteenpence.

A MANUAL

OF

STRUCTURAL BOTANY,

FOR THE USE OF

CLASSES, SCHOOLS, AND PRIVATE STUDENTS.

By M. C. COOKE.

ILLUSTRATED BY MORE THAN 200 ILLUSTRATIONS.

CONTENTS.

LONDON: ROBERT HARDWICKE, 192, PICCADILLY, W.

A MANUAL

OF

STRUCTURAL BOTANY.

LONDON : ROBERT HARDWICKE, 192, PICCADILLY, W.

www.ingramcontent.com/pod-product-compliance
Lightning Source LLC
Chambersburg PA
CBHW020628030726
47497CB00007B/2465